JIGSAW

JT LAWRENCE

FIRE FINCH

1

BLOOD RUNS COLD

49 GARDENIA AVENUE, **Greenside, Johannesburg, 11th of July 2014, 14:48.**

The wailing of the baby is a siren. Detective De Villiers shakes his aching head to dislodge the disconsolate howling which threatens to short-circuit his brain. He raises his voice. "You're the neighbour?"

The woman is distraught. She hasn't let go of the front of her blouse since the detective arrived, and the delicate fabric there is damp and wrinkled from the heat and moisture of her palm. She swallows and looks up at him. "Excuse me?"

"The neighbour. You're the neighbour who called this in?"

She nods and looks around as if the missing woman's kitchen will provide clues to her disappearance. "Yes."

"What made you call the police, Miss ... Digby?"

"Mrs Digby."

"Mrs Digby." Detective De Villiers makes a note in his Moleskine. It's an expensive notebook, one he could ill afford on his public service salary, but his wife had given it to him as a gift. It felt uncomfortable in his hands, which were used to cheap spiral-bound books from the stationery shelf at Pick n Pay. He scratches the ballpoint of his pen into the cream-coloured paper but stops mid-sentence. The howling is too much.

"Khaya!" he shouts. A fresh-faced sergeant jogs into the room.

"Sir?"

"Will you please do something with that child?"

The sergeant blinks. "Sir?"

"For God's sake, just take it outside or something. Play with it. Give it a toy or a bloody dummy or something."

He realises how barbed his voice is, but he can't think when his skull is on fire.

"You can't blame the baby for crying," says Mrs Digby.

"What?"

"I said, you can't blame the baby for crying. He's just a little thing. He's been abandoned! Who knows when last he was fed, or changed."

"Khaya!" shouts De Villiers.

"Detective?"

"Feed the kid, will you? Change his nappy."

The sergeant's eyes flare.

"Don't look at me like that! You have small kids at home. Don't tell me you've never changed a *fokken* nappy."

Khaya has the grace to look ashamed and murmurs his response. "I've never changed a *fokken* nappy."

De Villiers gives him a pointed look, then slams the Moleskine onto the kitchen counter. He opens a few cupboards until he finds what he's looking for. The detective spoons formula into a baby bottle and tops it up with warm water from the kettle. He pours a few drops of the milk onto his wrist, over the sink, and hands the bottle to the sergeant.

"I know what you're thinking," says Mrs Digby. "That I'm a bored housewife with nothing better to do than spy on my neighbours. But the crying just went on and on—"

De Villiers picks his notebook up again. "Nosy neighbours are a cop's best friend."

"I wasn't being nosy, I just ... I just can't believe she would do such a thing!"

"Who?"

"Emily! The mother. The woman who lives here."

The baby quietens down, and De Villiers feels his jaws unclench. "What do you mean, do such a thing? What is it you believe she has done?"

"It's quite clear, isn't it? Emily's taken off. She's abandoned her poor little baby."

He offers the distraught woman a seat at the kitchen table, a polished timber top with legs painted white. The scent of spicy citrus emanates from the fresh blood oranges in the fruit bowl. "When did you first become aware of the child crying?"

"It was lunchtime."

De Villiers looks up from his notes. "1 p.m.?"

"Yes, around then. I don't wear a watch. I was making myself a sandwich when I heard him. I didn't think much of it, I mean, babies cry. It never bothered us."

"So you would often hear him cry?"

"No, not often. Not often at all. In fact, when we bumped into each other, I'd tell Emily what a good baby he must be. She seemed like such a loving mother. I mean, I know she's a single mom, and that can't be easy, but she was always so tender towards him—"

"So why did you call the police this time?"

Mrs Digby finally lets go of her blouse, and the detective tries to ignore the patch of distressed fabric left behind. She taps her fingers lightly on the surface of the table. "Benjamin was crying when I made my lunch. I took it outside to eat on the patio, and when I brought my plate back to the kitchen, he was still crying."

"How much time had elapsed?"

"I'd say, maybe, half an hour?"

"Half an hour to eat a sandwich?"

"Five minutes to eat. But then I read a couple of chapters on my Kindle. Pulled out a few weeds."

"So, around 1:30 p.m.?" asks De Villiers.

"I think so. But the cries sounded different, like I'd never heard him cry before. He was really wailing. It made my blood run cold. I knew something was wrong. I rang the bell a few times, knocked on the door. Tried to phone her, but it just rang."

Khaya strolls into the kitchen, the baby asleep in his arms.

"Khaya!" says De Villiers. "How did you do that?"

"Shhh! He's only just fallen asleep."

"I'll be damned," says De Villiers. "Turns out you're a regular *fokken* baby-whisperer."

"Baby-what?" whispers the sergeant.

"Never mind, sergeant. My pounding head thanks you."

The doorbell rings. Khaya flinches and tries to shield the baby's ears, but it's too late, and soon new shrieks pierce the air.

Back in De Villiers' Toyota Hilux, the detective opens a rattling plastic bottle and shakes two pills out onto his palm. He chugs them down with a leftover sip of cold coffee from his travel mug. He grimaces at his reflection in the rear-view mirror, then stabs the ignition with his key.

"You should try the powder," says Khaya.

The detective sighs as he reverses. "What the bloody hell are you talking about?"

"Headache powder," says Khaya. "For your headache."

"You didn't have to say the last bit."

"Detective?"

"*For your headache*," says De Villiers. "You didn't have to say *for your headache* after saying headache powder when it's clear that I have a bloody headache."

"It's bad today, hey?"

"I expect I'll survive."

They drive for a while, De Villiers finally relaxing into the silence.

"So," ventures Khaya. "It looks like it's not a coincidence anymore."

De Villiers grunts in agreement.

"You taught me, Devil. There's no such thing as a coincidence."

The detective remains quiet, his mind whirring.

"Three babies abandoned, three mothers missing, in three weeks."

The detective smashes his indicator and makes a turn. "It doesn't make any sense, does it?"

"No one would bat an eyelid if they were black babies, you know?"

De Villiers heaves a sigh. "Yes, Khaya. We are all flaming racists, I know."

"I didn't mean it like that."

"How did you mean it?"

"I didn't mean anything. Only—"

"Only?"

"It's just ... sad. That's all."

De Villiers yanks the steering wheel and parks.

"What are we doing here?" Khaya asks, looking out of the window at the small corner shop.

"What do you think? I'm going to buy some *headache* powder. You want anything?"

"Nah, *dankie*."

"You sure?"

"Okay, maybe just a bar of chocolate."

The detective wrenches open his door and heads towards the shop. The pavement is potholed and strewn with skittering litter, like plastic tumbleweed.

Khaya winds down his window. "And a Coke!"

De Villiers turns back to the car and shields his scratchy eyes with his hand; the metallic glare is like a razor to his brain. He can still hear an echo of that baby crying. He's not sure he heard the sergeant correctly; had never seen him drink cola. "You want a Coke?"

"Not for me. For you! For the powder. It makes it work better."

2

GOD IS IN THE DETAILS

PARKVIEW POLICE STATION, **Johannesburg, 11th of July 2014, 16:28.**

A dozen cops wait for the briefing to start. Some are scrolling on their phones. A tall man unwraps a cheese roll; another pours lukewarm filter coffee. Determined footsteps enter the room, and the officers settle down.

"Hello people," says Major Alistair Denton.

The officers mumble their greetings.

"Okay, listen up," says Denton. "We have a sensitive one on our hands today."

"Let me guess," says Swanepoel, chewing. "A politician caught with his pants down?"

Some cops snigger, and the guy behind him swipes Swanepoel.

"*Eina!*" yells Swanepoel, almost dropping his roll. "*Jou moer.*"

"Thank you, Lieutenant Breytenbach," says the major.

Breytenbach grins. "Always a pleasure to hit Swanepoel, Major."

There is more sniggering, then the crowd hushes.

"As I was saying, we have a funny one. I've never seen anything like this before. I know you're all busy with your caseloads, but I need you to keep your eyes and ears open."

Breytenbach frowns. "You have our attention."

"Detective De Villiers will lead the case, and any help you can give him will be appreciated."

Swanepoel wipes his mouth with a paper serviette. "The Devil is beyond help, Major."

"That may be so, but we want all eyes on the ground nonetheless. If you come across anything—*anything*—that you think may pertain to the case, I want you to let De Villiers know about it."

The cops murmur their assent.

"Now the press doesn't know about this yet, they haven't connected the dots, but I'm sure they'll come sniffing around before long. It's going to be one of those cases that capture the public's imagination—and you know there's nothing I hate more than that."

"I'll hand over to De Villiers now." The major nods at the detective. "Tell this lot what they need to know."

Swanepoel chants. "Dev-il! Dev-il!"

"*Jussis* Swanepoel," says De Villiers. "If you're not careful, I'll get Breytenbach to re-arrange your face for you."

"It'll be an improvement," says Breytenbach.

"So hostile, De Villiers. Is that any way for a leading detective to talk?"

The detective stares at him for a moment, and then looks away, but not before he notices a slight red smudge on Swanepoel's collar.

"Shut up, will you?" says Vellie. "I've got work to do. I can feel my cases cooling as I speak."

De Villiers clears his throat and holds up the new file in his hand. "We were called to the house of another abandoned baby today."

"What now? They've got the Devil babysitting?" Swanepoel whistles. "What is the world coming to?"

De Villiers ignores the jibe. "So, for those not paying attention: that's three white babies abandoned in Jo'burg in the last three weeks. All the missing persons—"

"—the mothers—" says Khaya.

"Yes, the mothers. They have things in common. All three of them are in their thirties, and all three are single. Decent incomes, supportive families."

"So you're saying no reason to run?" says Breytenbach.

"No apparent reason, which is different."

Khaya pipes up. "They all packed a suitcase, clothes, underwear, toiletries, and some valuables. And no sign of forced entry at any of the homes."

"And they didn't know each other?" asks Breytenbach.

"It doesn't look like it. But we're still trying to find a link."

"There'll be a link," says Devil.

"And what about their activities after leaving?" asks Swanepoel. "Paper-trail?"

De Villiers shakes his head. "None. No plane tickets, no cash drawn from ATMs, no credit card transactions."

"So they don't want to be found."

"Either that, or ..."

"Either that or they've been taken."

"Seems like an odd thing to do," says Swanepoel. "Abduct three seemingly unrelated mothers, leaving the babies behind. Usually, it's the other way around. At least you can sell a baby. Or three babies."

Devil's mouth turns down at the corners. "It won't be three for long."

Breytenbach stops fidgeting. "You think he's a serial?"

"No one said the mothers are dead," says Swanepoel. "They're probably on the run or something. Maybe they've had enough of their babies and everything and decided to just *sommer* up and leave. Joined a cult or something. Maybe they're all together at some kind of hot yoga retreat doing headstands and drinking kombucha somewhere in the bloody Himalayas."

The police officers laugh.

De Villiers bangs the desk loudly to get everyone's attention. "I think it's a serial killer."

The crowd quietens down. The sergeant doesn't try to hide his glee. "My first serial killer!"

The detective shakes his head. "Don't get ahead of yourself, Khaya. I might be wrong."

Swanepoel snorts.

"What is it, Swanepoel? You think I'm never wrong?"

"No, I think you never think you're wrong."

They stare at each other for a moment.

"A serial killer?" says Breytenbach, breaking the tension. "It is a bit of a stretch."

"A serial killer who is invited in and also nicely packs his victims' bags for them?" says Swanepoel. "I think you're dreaming."

"It's just a hunch," says Devil. "We won't know anything unless we get off our arses and get some investigating done. I'd appreciate it if all of you just kept your eyes open on this one. I have a feeling that a fourth baby will be 'abandoned' very soon, and I'd like very much to stop that from happening. Vellie and Breytenbach, check out the mothers. Any pertinent background info, but look especially for anything that links them together. A playgroup, a nanny, an ex-boyfriend. Look at the fathers of the kids. Why aren't they on the scene? Swanepoel and Modise, I need you to focus on forensics. Was it really no forced entry? Maybe they packed their own bags, maybe they didn't. You need to find out. The rest of you, just keep your eyes open and your brain switched on. Any detail, people, even if you think it's irrelevant, if you come across any little thing, come to me. Cases like this are solved by paying attention to—"

"Details," says Khaya.

"Details," says Breytenbach.

"Exactly," says De Villiers, tapping the bottom of the file on the desk in front of him. Chairs scrape the floor and pens click closed as the cops get ready to leave the briefing room.

"And no one is to breathe a word of this outside this station, got it?"

The major sticks his head around the corner, his silver hair catching the harsh light of the fluorescent tubes overhead. "De Villiers? I need you in my office, pronto."

De Villiers' lips are a hard line. He jerks his head, indicating Khaya should join them.

Major Alistair Denton's office is humble, but when the door is closed, it's a welcome quiet sanctuary from the perennial buzzing of the police station. De Villiers places his hand on the back of an old chair, ready to pull it out.

"Don't bother sitting," says Denton. "This will only take a minute. Top-line, what can you tell me?"

"Never heard of anything like this before," says detective De Villiers.

"You don't think these women left of their own accord?"

"It would be strange if they did."

"Look, I'll be honest," says the major. "I've got a feeling about this case."

"What kind of feeling?"

"A bad one. This is just the beginning of a shitstorm. I need you two to be completely focused on this, you hear me? I want you to eat and breathe this case. I doubt you'll have time to sleep, but if you do, I want you to dream about this case. You got it?"

The men nod.

Denton takes a breath, then sighs it out. "Look, I didn't want to ask this, but I have to. De Villiers, are you up for it? You know, I understand if you need some personal time."

"Yes, Major. Up for it, one hundred per cent."

"I know it must be difficult, with your—"

"Not at all, Major."

Alastair looks satisfied. "I'm counting on you, De Villiers. You're the best I have."

The major's phone rings; he picks up the receiver. "Denton." He listens to the caller while De Villiers notices a patch of red bloom on the major's neck. "Damn it," he says. "Who? From where? What? ECN? Well, who the hell told her? I swear I'm going to—"

Devil whispers to Khaya. "I think that's our cue."

"Just a second," Denton says into the phone, then looks up at De

Villiers and Khaya. "Hey, you two. Either of you know a Jennifer Walker? A journalist?"

They shake their heads, and he waves them away.

"Listen," Denton yells down the line. "I don't know who she's been talking to, but it's no one at my station. There's no evidence to support the theory that it's a serial killer." Khaya closes the door softly as they leave.

"That's interesting," says De Villiers.

"What is?"

"That within minutes of leaving the briefing room, a certain journalist knew about my hunch."

"Do you know her?" asks Khaya. "The journalist?"

"Not personally, but I can tell you that she wears a very bright shade of red lipstick."

Khaya stops walking. "Hey?"

"Details, sergeant. God is in the details. Or in this case, not God but an ambitious young journalist named Jennifer Walker.

Khaya's confused.

"It was Swanepoel, man."

"Hey? She must be *helluva* ambitious to be sleeping with Swanepoel for information."

"Agreed."

"Are you going to report him to the major?"

"No," says De Villiers, walking ahead. "Best keep it to ourselves. It may come in handy."

3

STECHKIN, SAIGA

ROSENDAL, **the Free State, 12th of July 2014, 07:06.**

Early morning sun streams into the farm kitchen, transforming dust motes to fine glitter. Robin Susman, stiff from the morning's work with the lambs, prepares her modest breakfast. One just-laid egg—a gift from her Lohmann Brown hen named Scribble—boils on the old gas stovetop. She pops a slice of home-style buttermilk bread into the toaster and wipes the crumbs off her fingers. In the distance, sheep make themselves heard. Robin closes her eyes for a moment, enjoying the serenity which she believes she'll never take for granted. When the phone in the hall rings, the sound is jarring. She makes her way over to the old-fashioned appliance, the wooden floorboards creaking beneath her.

"Hello?"

"Robin, darling," purrs an affectionate female voice.

Anxiety turns to delight. "Clem! Is that you?"

"The one and only. Sorry for the sparrows-fart call, but I know you farmer-types are up earlier than the rest of us go to bed."

"No problem at all," says Robin. She can't help smiling. "Lovely to hear your voice."

"I know you gave up your cell phone. And your inbox. So I didn't know how else to reach you."

"It's no problem, Clementine, really. As you say, I've been up for hours—"

"Well, I won't keep you, darling, I just wanted to—"

"Did something happen? Are you okay?"

It's one downfall of being an ex-detective. You always expect news to be bad.

"Yes! God, yes. All okay on this side. The kids are a complete handful. I don't know what I was thinking, having three."

Too much chardonnay, she used to joke. *Not enough contraception.*

"Hang on," says Robin. She sets the receiver down on the side table and runs to the kitchen to grab her tea, then settles into the chair near the phone. The springs squeak as she shifts in it, trying to get comfortable. Like Robin Susman, the chair has seen better days.

"The kids must be so big now!"

"They are. It's an utter circus here on a good day. But you know what they say. Thank God for nannies and gin."

Robin laughs; it feels good. There is an intimate pause in the conversation as she draws her legs up and twists the phone cord around her fingers. "You should come to visit again, you know. You're always welcome. Bring the kids. I've got loads of space here. I'd love to see them, and I'm sure they'd love the farm. Adore the lambs. They can run around with the local kids and the chickens. Play soccer or something. Get dirty. Maybe pick up some Zulu."

"Visit?" asks Clementine, feigning shock. "I thought you were too busy being a hermit. I thought you didn't want any visitors. In fact, I heard through the grapevine that you shoot visitors on sight."

"You're not a 'visitor'. You're my dearest friend and always welcome here."

"Fancy that," says Clementine.

"What?"

"You. Being a farmer. Raising sheep."

"I know. It's been three years, and I'm still not entirely sure what I'm doing."

"My God, Robin, I wouldn't know the first thing about sheep!"

"I mean, I don't know what I'm doing with my life." Robin takes a sip of her tea. It's cold.

"Don't we all, darling? Some days I'm not sure if I'm Arthur or Martha. But I'm sure it can get lonely out there, all on your own. It's so quiet. I'm sure your thoughts can drive you crazy."

"Yes, it's quiet," says Robin. "But in a good way. Peaceful."

"You don't miss the bright city lights?"

"God, no. The only dreams I have of that place are nightmares."

"You don't miss being a hot-shot cop?"

"Ha. No."

"So what do you do? You know, with sheep? If my closest friend is determined to be a sheep farmer, I need to know something about it, at the very least."

"Well. It turns out I'm not very good at sheep farming, after all," sighs Robin.

"I don't believe that for a moment. You've always been good at anything you tried. I'm sure the sheep are no match for you."

"Seriously," says Robin, laughing. "I'm a terrible farmer. It's the lambing."

"The what?"

She stops laughing. "The lambing. The lambs! I can't bear to send them to the abattoir."

"God, I didn't even consider that."

"I didn't think it would be a problem. In theory, it wasn't a problem. I was so used to seeing bloodshed—"

"Ah, Rob."

"But after ... after it happened, I just can't face any more violence."

"Of course you can't."

"And they're so dear, Clementine, you should see them. They're so lovely. And I put so much time and effort into rearing them—"

"You become attached."

"I fed some of them by bottle, you know, when they were just babies. The little ones that got bullied by the bigger ones."

"Oh darling," says Clementine. "You've named them, haven't you?"

"Of course I have! They're my pets, now."

"You've turned into a big softie, Detective Robin Susman. I never thought I'd see the day."

"Ex-detective," Robin replies. "And I am certainly not a 'softie'. I named them after Russian firearms. Tokarev, Makarov, Stechkin, Saiga."

Clementine shrieks with laughter. "You're pulling my leg."

"I am not." Robin abandons her mug on the side table. "There's also Simonov. He's the one with the funny ear. And Dragunov. I sleep with a shotgun next to my pillow."

"Now that's more like it. The Robin Susman I know and love."

Susman sighs. "Although I use the term 'sleep' loosely."

"Still having the nightmares?"

"It's difficult to fall asleep when you know what's waiting for you on the other side."

"You still going for therapy?"

"Counselling? Yawn. Yes. We Skype every Wednesday at two."

"Skype? So you're not the tech-troglodyte you purport to be. Is it helping?"

"The short answer is no. I mean, it's been over three years already. I need to get over it. Move past it. Sometimes I think the counselling just reminds me. Keeps me stuck—I don't know—I mean, that's why I took down all the mirrors in the house."

"You ... what?"

"Because I was being reminded of what happened every day. I have enough scars on the inside without having to look at the ones on the outside, too." Robin takes a deep breath. "Anyway—as I said—I need to get over it already."

"Does one ever get over something like that?"

Robin thinks about it, then shakes her head. "Probably not." She hears a cracking sound in the kitchen. "Shit! I forgot about the stove! I've got to go. Thanks for the catch-up!"

"Wait!" yells Clementine. "I won't keep you much longer, but I almost forgot the reason I called you."

The water had probably evaporated by now, and the egg would have split in two, or exploded.

"Yes?"

"You're not going to like it."

"Land the plane, Clem! My kitchen is probably burning down as we speak."

"It's Alistair," she says.

Suddenly, a burning kitchen doesn't seem very important. "Clementine," she says, carefully. "I know you have nothing but good intentions, but I don't want to talk about Alistair."

"It's not what you think. I've given up trying to get you guys back together."

"Thank God. At last. What changed?"

"He ... oh, never mind. Best if he tells you himself."

"He won't," Robin says. "We don't talk."

"Oh, I know that. That's why I'm calling, you see. I needed to warn you—"

"Sounds ominous," says Robin, twisting the phone cord tighter.

"They're coming to get you, darling."

"What now?"

"My esteemed brother, Major Alistair Denton. He's going to ask his top cop to visit you at the farm. Hopefully, bring you back for a short while. There's a case—"

Robin grinds her teeth. "Tell him not to waste the guy's time. There is no way I'm going back to Jo'burg."

"That's what I told him. But apparently, it's just your kind of case—"

"Absolutely not. No way."

"That's exactly what I said, I promise. I said they'd just waste their time. But you know Alistair."

Robin sighs. "Yes, I know Alistair."

"Once he's got an idea in his head..."

"Yes."

"I'm sorry, darling. I did everything I could to put him off, short of lying."

"What do you mean, short of lying?"

"Well, he started the conversation asking how you were. He gave me the idea that if you weren't, you know, *well*, then he wouldn't bother you. But you're good, aren't you, darling? I mean, you're better. You're doing well now."

"Apart from insomnia and nightmares, you mean? Panic attacks?"

Clementine's voice falls in dismay. "I didn't know about those."

"Don't worry. If they come, I'll just send them on their way. Thanks for the warning. I appreciate it. Really, I do. Now I need to—"

"Can we seriously come and visit? The whole monstrous family, Pete included? If he can get some time off? I'll bring you a trove of city supplies. Whatever you like, that you can't get there. Hair products? Body butter? *Touche éclat*? Nespresso pods?"

"Clem, have you ever known me to use a hair product?"

"Sorry! I do get carried away."

"And a Nespresso machine has no place on a farm in the Free State. We drink *moerkoffie* here."

"At the risk of sounding like a snob, darling, that sounds awful. I may have to bring my machine along and hide it in the cupboard in my room, along with my bottle of gin. No one will have to know."

Susman pauses. "I'd kill for a croissant. You know, a real one. Not the abominations they sell here in town."

"I'll bring you a dozen! We'll eat two every morning."

"'That sounds wonderful."

"You start making a list. Your wish is my command. Call me when you're ready."

"I will. Oh, and Clem—"

"Yes?"

"Do me a favour?"

"Anything."

"Re-direct your warning to Alistair. Tell him if he sends his troops, I'll be waiting for them. With my shotgun."

4

ORPHAN

A WOMAN WHIMPERS. Her whole body shakes as if she's trapped inside a vehicle riding over cobblestones, instead of where she is: in a dank, claustrophobic room where everything is dark and cold and still. The air stinks of sourness and evil. Heavy footsteps arrive outside the locked door, and the wrenching open of the sliding bolt sounds like a gunshot. She can't control her shaking.

The silhouette scrapes open the door, flooding the tiny room with yellow light. Emily has to close her eyes against the bright ache. Her kidnapper lunges down, and she feels a ripping pain on her lips and cheeks. He pockets the grimy duct tape that had been keeping her silent.

"I'm so cold," she mutters. She's desperate. "I'm so cold. Why is it so cold in here? Please. I think I might die."

She feels as if her skeleton is frozen lead. Icy and numb, but not numb enough to stop the stinging feeling where her bare skin meets the cold concrete.

"Keep quiet," warns the man, "or I'll put the tape back on."

Sobs bubble up Emily's throat; she tries to swallow them. She doesn't want to make him angry. "Please," she begs. "I need to get back to my baby."

He punches the brick wall. His knuckles come away wet with fresh blood. "I said, shut up!"

"He needs me," says Emily. She feels the dirt on her face.

The man shoves a scuffed plastic bottle up to her face. "Drink. Quickly. Then the tape is going back on."

She drinks greedily as he angles the bottle for her. Some water drips onto her chest, which she knows will make her colder still. She doesn't know if she will survive it.

"Why are you doing this?" she asks, as if having a reason will make it more bearable. "Where is Benjamin?"

The man's voice is gruff and reeks with depravity. "Benjamin is fine. He'll be an orphan, soon."

Emily cries. She's tired and weak, having tried everything she can to escape the binding on her wrists and ankles. Her hands are bleeding from trying to saw the rope on the rough brick wall.

"He'll be okay," says the man. "I was an orphan, too. And look, I turned out just fine."

5

A SECRET WEAPON

PARKVIEW POLICE STATION, **Johannesburg, 12th of July 2014, 10:28.**

The police station is a hive. A television flickers in the background. Sergeant Khaya strides up to De Villiers' desk. "They've put Benjamin in a place of safety, sir. He's doing okay."

The detective looks up, his mind as blank as a new Etch-a-Sketch. "Benjamin?"

"The baby, from yesterday. Greenside."

"You didn't have to say 'Greenside', Khaya."

"I was just—"

"If there were two babies yesterday, in different locations, then it would make sense to say 'Greenside.'"

"Sorry. Sometimes I just talk before I think."

"You and the rest of the world." He takes a sip from the water bottle on his desk. "But I'm glad the kid is safe. Breytenbach!"

Lieutenant Breytenbach spins on his heels, changing direction to face De Villiers. *"Yebo?"*

"Anything linking those three mothers yet?"

"Not yet."

"You're not trying hard enough," says Devil.

"I've tried every link I can think of so far for three white ladies in Jozi. Boyfriends, book clubs, wine clubs, bird clubs, alumni, universities, schools. Spas. Doctors, midwives. I checked out which hospitals they had their babies in."

"Anything in common there?"

"Two of the three babies were born at the Sandton hospital. The other one at, like, a hippie place."

De Villiers looks at the lieutenant. "A what?"

"You know, like a natural birthing place."

Khaya frowns. "Aren't all births natural?"

"Khaya," chuckles De Villiers. "What you know about the fairer sex is ... well, it's scary."

Swanepoel chokes on his coffee and almost spits it out his nose.

Khaya clicks his tongue in annoyance. "Shut up, Swanepoel."

"Check if they went to the same antenatal classes, or are in post-natal groups or something. Baby gym, baby maths, that kind of thing."

Something catches the detective's eye. "Hold on a second. Turn up the volume on that TV."

Vellie, who has the remote, turns up the sound. It's a news program. The anchor's face is a mask, devoid of emotion. He's so used to the brutal headlines he doesn't feel the tragedy anymore. "Another rocket attack in Palestine in the early hours of this morning took the fatality tally in the Middle East up to 746 this month."

"*Yussis*," says De Villiers.

"An estimated seventy per cent of the deaths in Palestine have been civilians, mostly women and children."

De Villiers sighs and rubs his face.

Khaya looks worried. "Still no word from Niel?"

"Nothing since these bloody attacks started again, three weeks ago."

"He should be pretty safe there, though?" says Breytenbach. "The kibbutzim aren't near the Gaza strip. Plus, they have the Iron Dome."

"It's not that simple," says Devil.

Breytenbach nods. "Sure, I get it. If I had a son, I wouldn't want him anywhere near there."

"They get leave, you know. The kibbutz workers get time off, and they travel a bit. We can't get hold of him or the kibbutz people. He could be anywhere. He could be—"

"Oh, shit," says Swanepoel, eyeing the screen.

Breytenbach turns to him. "What now?"

They tune in to the news anchor once again. "And in local news, the mothers of the three abandoned babies have yet to be found. In what at first appeared to be a bizarre coincidence, Sandra Longman, Desiree van Zyl, and Emily Shuter disappeared a week apart, leaving their infants behind. There was no sign of forced entry at their homes and some of their clothes, toiletries, and valuables were also missing, leading authorities to believe that they had left of their own accord—"

"Bullshit," says Swanepoel.

"—But subsequent facts have come to light, indicating that there may be more to the story than simple abandonment. Meanwhile, members of the public have been protesting outside police stations in Diepsloot and Alexandra this morning. Jennifer Walker is there."

The picture on the television cuts to shaky live footage of a protest in Diepsloot. People are singing and shouting; previous footage shows a shop being looted. A beautiful journalist holding a microphone comes into view. "Tell us why you are protesting today."

The protestor has to shout to be heard above the ruckus. "We want the government to know that we are not stupid!"

"What do you mean by that?" asks Jennifer Walker.

"They think we are stupid because we are poor. They think they can take advantage of us. Give us no security, no police. They don't care. They don't care about our babies."

"Do you mean, abandoned babies?"

"Yes! Do you know there are babies left here every day. Do the police care? No. Do the newspapers care? No. Black babies don't matter."

"You're upset because if a black baby is abandoned, no one cares, but if a white baby is abandoned, it makes the news."

"That is what I am saying."

"Oh please," says Breytenbach. "That journalist set that up."

"Doesn't make it untrue," says Khaya.

The major arrives at the doorway, his face like thunder, and Vellie turns the volume down again. "De Villiers, Khaya, in my office now."

As they follow the major, Swanepoel whistles as if they are schoolboys on their way to the headmaster's office.

Major Alastair Denton's phone rings. "Denton," he barks. "Yes. Yes, damn it. Just do it. Don't ask permission. Do it and apologise after-wards, if you have to." He replaces the receiver with a little more force than necessary, then looks pointedly at his men. "I can handle the pressure from above, and the protests and the irresponsible press snapping at my heels. But I can't stand these young mothers being held somewhere." He shakes his head. "God knows what is being done to them."

His eyes travel to the framed photograph of his wife and baby on his desk. "You need to save them. And if it's too late to save them, then at least stop more from going missing."

"We're doing everything we can, Major. We'll stop this guy. It's just a matter of time."

"There's something else," says Denton. "I need you to ... drive to Rosendal."

De Villiers stares incredulously. "Rosendal? In the Free State?"

"Yes, in the Free State," says Denton. "First thing tomorrow morning."

"But, Major, we need to be *here*. You said 'no distractions'!"

"This is not a distraction," says the major. "This will help you solve the case. Think of it—think of *her*—as a secret weapon."

Khaya's head shoots up like a mongoose. "Her?"

De Villiers sighs in defeat. "Detective Robin Susman."

The major corrects him. "Ex-detective Susman."

Khaya looks from the major to De Villiers, then back again. "Who?"

"What is she doing in Rosendal? Can't she just drive to the city herself?"

"It's not as simple as just picking her up. You need to convince her to come with you, back to Jo'burg, to help solve this case."

De Villiers laughs, then stops. "You're kidding."

"Be assured that I am not."

"Can't you just call her?" asks Devil. "Can't you convince her? I mean, I haven't seen her in ages. You two used to be friends."

"We used to be close, yes. But she won't listen to me. Not about this."

"Forgive me, Major, but it sounds like a bit of a lost cause, and we don't have time to waste."

"I wouldn't send you men if I didn't absolutely believe that she is imperative to solving this case."

"Why? Why would she have an advantage over us? She's been out of the force for years."

"Robin Susman is an excellent detective," says Denton.

De Villiers stares at him. "Robin Susman *used* to be an excellent detective."

"You know as well as I do that she has a knack with these kinds of cases. I know. I saw it over and over again when we worked together. Don't take it personally, De Villiers. It's not that she's better than you. She's just ... different. She'll bring a different perspective and skill-set to the investigation." He tears a page from his block of notepaper and hands it to Khaya.

"Will you at least phone her and tell her to expect us?" asks De Villiers.

The major laughs, but there is no happiness or humour in the sound. "If I did that, she'd be long gone by the time you got there."

Breytenbach's phone vibrates on his desk. He swears in a low voice and snatches it up, then carries it outside to the busy pavement where no one will overhear the conversation.

"Breytenbach here."

The distorted voice of the caller replies. "Erol Breytenbach."

Breytenbach looks around. "Yes, it's me."

"Your payment is late," says the robotic voice.

There is a slight sheen on his forehead. "Yes, I know. I'm sorry. I'm trying to get it together."

"Don't jerk me around, Breytenbach."

"I'm not! I'm not, I swear. I just had some unexpected expenses this month."

"Not my problem."

"I know!" he shouts, then looks around again and lowers his voice.

"You'll pay by the end of the day today, or our agreement comes to an end."

"Please, I just need a few more days. I just need—"

The line goes dead, leaving Breytenbach to stare at the traffic that streams incessantly past the police station. He spends a minute thinking, kicks a small rock, then makes his way back into the orange-bricked building. Swanepoel is hanging out at the front desk, flirting with a female sergeant, his tall frame spilling over the varnished oak surface. "Hey, Breytenbach."

Breytenbach's not in the mood to deal with him and shoots Swanepoel a warning look.

"Whoa," says Swanepoel, raising his hands in mock surrender. "Who pissed on your rainbow?"

At the same time, De Villiers storms out of the major's office, and Khaya tries to keep up.

"Hey," says Swanepoel. "Why is everyone so the *moer* in?"

De Villiers and Breytenbach yell at the same time. "Shut up, Swanepoel!"

6

GOOD RIDDANCE

N1, **Senekal, the Free State, 13th of July 2014, 09:16.**

"It's nice," says Khaya, looking out of the car window. There's not a cloud in the sky, and the air is dry. The road stretches for miles before them, cutting through the field of golden grass.

"*Ja*," says De Villiers. "Coldplay. Have you seen them live?"

"No, I meant, this place."

The detective grunts. "What's nice about it?"

"The open spaces. The grass."

Devil shoots the sergeant a contemptuous look. "The *grass*?"

"The veld. You know what I mean, Captain. It's nice to be out of the city. I miss it, you know. The open spaces."

"No one is keeping you in Jo'burg, Khaya. If you're so bloody homesick then you should go back to doing ... whatever it was you were doing before you moved to sin city."

Khaya doesn't reply; he watches as birds perch on twisted cables like black liquorice. There is a pause in the conversation, and De Villiers realises he has been too harsh with the sergeant, and not for the first time.

"So," he says, lightly. "You don't like the music?"

"Not my style."

"Chris Martin is an incredibly talented musician."

"To be honest," says the sergeant. "I never pegged you for a Coldplay fan."

"Well, you know what they say. Every day is a school day."

"*Askies?*"

"You know, you learn something every day. Never mind. It's just a saying. My mother used to say it. She was a teacher."

"I thought maybe you'd like some *boeremusiek*," says Khaya, a smile reaching his eyes.

De Villiers looks offended. "What's that now?"

"You know, Gé Carstens."

The detective scoffs. "You mean Nico Carstens? Or Gé Korsten?"

"Ja, those guys. And Steve Hofmeyr."

"Hofmeyr?" laughs De Villiers. "*Is jy mal?*"

Khaya snorts with laughter. "Just kidding, sir."

There is another break in conversation, but now the atmosphere in the car is light. De Villiers notices how red the soil is and thinks the landscape is quite pleasant, after all.

"So," says Khaya. "You know this lady, this Detective Susman?"

"Ex-detective," says De Villiers. "And she's no lady."

"You've worked with her?"

De Villiers nods. "She was a good cop. A damn good cop."

"I was asking around at the station. I heard she's a feminist."

Devil chortles. "Oh bugger off, Khaya."

"No, seriously, sir. That's what they were saying."

"And what the hell do you know about feminism, Khaya? Wait, don't answer that. And don't bring it up with Susman either, you got it?"

"Why?"

"Because she'll have your balls for breakfast, that's why."

"I'm just ... interested, that's all."

De Villiers whacks his steering wheel in mirth. "Interested? In feminism? The man who thinks changing nappies is women's work? Pull the other one."

"Is she a lesbian?"

"Holy shit, Khaya. Not that it's any of your business, but no, she's not. And don't you dare say anything like that to her."

"Does she hate men?"

"Probably. And if she does, it's with good reason."

"Why did she leave the job? If she was so good?"

The amusement fades from De Villiers' face. "Something happened. Something terrible happened to her when she was working a case. And that's also none of your business."

"But," says Khaya, "you will have to tell me so I don't say the wrong thing."

De Villiers exhales.

"You know me, Captain. Perennial foot-in-mouth disease."

The detective purses his lips. "Don't I know it."

De Villiers spots the sign for the off-ramp and indicates to exit. When they're off the highway and stationary at a red traffic light, he clears his throat. "Susman was the best detective in the squad. She was so good that they even let her choose her own cases. Towards the end, she was only working on cases where the victims were women. Gender-based violence: that was her thing. She worked her arse off—overtime, nights, weekends—she was always on the job, like if she worked hard enough, she could keep women from getting hurt. They promoted her left, right and centre. Youngest cop ever to make detective. But she was also heading towards burn-out, everyone could see it."

De Villiers accelerates into a left turn, and they fly down a tree-lined lane which turns into a sand road. Stones crunch and pop under the Hilux tyres.

"Have you ever heard of the Turbine Hall Gang?"

"It sounds familiar—"

"There was this gang—five men—they used to operate in the CBD and the Parks. They terrorised people. Hijacking, rape, murder. They were reckless. Ruthless. If someone got in their way, they would just kill them. The one vic was a fifteen-year-old boy. He was trying to protect his mother from them, and they just shot him in the neck."

Khaya blanches.

"The gang got more and more brazen. They thought they could never get caught."

"And Susman caught them?"

De Villiers puts his foot down as if driving faster would help get the story told. "We'd get one of their rape victims in the station every week. Susman couldn't take it. It became an obsession with her. As if she felt responsible for the attacks. Every new victim was an indictment. It was like she didn't care about anything apart from the Turbine Hall Gang. She needed to stop them."

They approach the entrance to a large property awash with white wildflowers. A small steel signpost swings in the breeze. The sign is blank.

"This is it. Turn in here."

When they reach the farm-style gate, Khaya hops out to drag it open for the vehicle.

"I love farms," says Khaya. "Look at these trees. Sheep! Look, Devil, sheep! Hello, sheep!"

"Hells bells, Khaya, what are you, five years old?"

Khaya stops prancing around and looks up towards the house; a large, rambling estate with a wraparound porch. "Hey, is that her?"

"Where?" asks De Villiers, trying to visualise the house from behind the dusty windscreen and failing.

"There, on the *stoep*."

De Villiers slows the Toyota to a stop and kills the engine.

"What is she holding?" asks Khaya.

The detective finally catches sight of her. He's taken aback. Robin Susman looks feral, with a wild mane of hair, and she's holding a shot-gun. She lifts it in both hands and fires a warning shot into the air.

De Villiers jumps. "What the hell?"

Susman walks towards them. "This is private property!"

The detective opens his door slowly and steps out, hands in the air. "Susman!" he yells. "It's me! Devil! André!"

"Get back in your car, De Villiers! Get back in your car and get off my land!"

Khaya, spooked, leaps back into the car. "You heard her, let's go!"

"Five minutes, Robin, please! We just drove all the way from—"

"Move out De Villiers!" She loads her shotgun again. "The next one won't be a warning shot!"

"Devil!" urges Khaya.

"Look," shouts De Villiers, hands still raised. "I don't want to upset you."

"Too late!" she yells, smoothing her wild hair away from her face. "You have upset me. You've upset an unbalanced woman with a loaded shotgun. Best you don't stick around."

"We just need—"

Susman points her gun at the car and keeps advancing. She squints along the barrel.

"Oh, shit," murmurs Khaya.

"Get back in your car, Devil," she growls. "And don't come back!"

"Susman. We won't leave until—"

Susman fires again. Buckshot ricochets off the hard ground, of rocks, and an empty, rusted metal barrel. De Villiers curses and dives behind the steering wheel, reversing as fast as he can. She reloads and fires once more, which hits the pole a meter from De Villiers' head. Robin Susman muses that if she were also in the habit of naming her ammunition, that particular shell would have been called Good Riddance.

7

UNLUCKY WORLD

ROSENDAL, the Free State, 13th of July 2014, 09:59.

"I have an idea," says De Villiers.

"If your idea is to get off Susman's property right now and drive back to Jo'burg, then I think it is a very good idea."

The men hunch down in the car, breathing hard, shaken up. De Villiers isn't sure if it's his imagination, but he thinks he hears sheep bleating.

"No," says De Villiers.

"She's *mal!*" cries Khaya. *"Hlanya!* She almost shot us!"

"She was trying to scare us away. She's not a real threat."

"You're as crazy as she is," says the sergeant. "That gun was real. The shot were real! I almost caught one in my leg!"

"Believe me, Khaya, if Robin Susman wanted to shoot you, you'd be bleeding."

"Have you considered that maybe she really *is* mad? Maybe she's not the same cop you used to know."

"Possibly," concedes De Villiers. "But we can't go back to the station without her. The major will sling us out on our backsides. Pass me the file."

Khaya looks around for the case file, which had been thrown around in the battle. He retrieves it from the back seat, neatens it up, and hands it to De Villiers. The detective takes a breath and climbs out of the car, then ducks his head back into the vehicle cabin. "Here, take my phone. Wait for one minute, then call this number. Make conversation."

"Hey?" says Khaya, wide-eyed. "Whose number is it? Devil? Where are you going? I'm telling you, you're going to get shot!"

"*Ja*, well," he says, with swagger that he doesn't feel. "It won't be the first time."

The detective makes his way up the dusty driveway. A minute later, he hears an old telephone ring from deep inside the house. Once it's answered, he darts up to the front entrance and quickly posts the photos of the missing mothers under the door. He sits against the wall and waits. The receiver is slammed down and Susman's footsteps return, slowing when they see the pictures on the floor. De Villiers hears movement and a sigh, and guesses she has sat down right there. He can feel her presence on the other side of the door. After a while, she speaks. Her voice is muffled.

"Who are they?"

De Villiers hesitates.

"Devil, I know you're on the other side of this door."

"Can we talk?" asks De Villiers

"Who are these women?"

"Sandra, Desiree, Emily. They've been ... abducted."

"Why did you hesitate there?"

"What?"

"You hesitated. Before you said *abducted*."

"I'm not sure. I'm not sure what happened to them. They have disappeared."

"They're dead," says Susman.

"Yes, I think so."

De Villiers scrubs his hair with his knuckles. "Hard to say, without bodies."

"It's a serial killer," repeats Susman. It hadn't been a question. "What links these women, apart from their looks?"

"All young mothers. Single mothers. All left a small baby boy behind."

"All packed a suitcase?" asks Susman.

"Yes, how did you know?"

"He wanted to make it look like they took off. Abandoned their babies. That was important to him."

There is a long pause, and De Villiers wonders if Susman will say anything else. Then her voice returns, filled with emotion.

"Can you imagine?" she asks. "Can you imagine being torn away from a new baby when you are that baby's universe? You are its everything. And then ... then you're nothing."

"Listen, Robin. This case has got your name written all over it."

"I left that all behind," she replies. "I don't want my name written on anything anymore. Especially not something like this."

De Villiers clenches his jaw. "Too bad."

"I guess so."

"Well, the major won't let us go back without you. We must stay here. Camp out with your cattle."

"Sheep. They're sheep, damn it. Can't you hear them?"

"We can't leave without you, and the longer it takes for you to come with us, the longer we take away from the case. We need to get back. We need to stop this guy from taking another mother away from her child."

"I won't be manipulated," she says.

"Fine," sighs Devil. "Then, don't be manipulated. It doesn't change the fact that you are one of the few people who can stop this guy."

Eventually, he hears her stand up, so he does the same, dusting the seat of his pants. The red soil, the orange dust, gets everywhere. Susman unlocks it and bangs the screen door open.

"Is that your way of inviting me in?" asks De Villiers.

Susman crosses her arms. "It's the closest to an invitation you're going to get."

~

Parkview Police Station, Johannesburg, 13th of July 2014, 13:08.

Major Alastair Denton's phone rings. He drops his pen, rubs his face, then answers.

"Denton."

"Is this a secure line?"

"Wait." He pushes a button. "Now, it is." He pauses. "Smith. Don't take this the wrong way, but you are absolutely the last person I wanted to hear from this week."

"Hey, you're the one paying me."

"As I said, don't take it personally." He rotates in his chair. "What do you have?"

"The Turbine Hall Gang."

Denton's stomach seizes. "No."

"Nasty buggers. I did some reading on them after you briefed me."

"Since when do you read?" asks the major.

"Since ... Google."

The major pinches the bridge of his nose. "Okay. What's new?"

"They're applying for early parole."

"Impossible."

"Nope," says Smith. "Not impossible. They filed the papers this morning. Can I ask you something?"

"What?"

"If they did all that stuff—those gang rapes. Murder. Killed that young boy. Why were they only given a seven-year sentence?"

Denton tries to swallow the lump of anxiety in his throat, but it won't budge. "The police-work."

Smith sounds surprised. "Bad police-work?"

"No," says the major. "Excellent police-work, but the evidence was ... compromised."

"How?"

"None of your business. Not for now, anyway."

"So, what do you want me to do?"

Denton thinks for a moment. "Sit tight for now. Keep me informed. If we need to ... take steps, I'll let you know."

"It doesn't make much sense, does it?"

"What?"

"That a rhino poacher gets seventy-seven years in prison, but these guys get seven."

"They were only found guilty of illegal possession of firearms. We didn't get them on anything else."

"They got lucky."

"We got ... unlucky," replies the major.

He hears Smith sigh. "It's an unlucky world."

8

MACABRE FAIRY GODMOTHER

ROSENDAL, **the Free State, 13th of July 2014, 15:04.**

Susman sulks in the passenger seat. Khaya has been relegated to the rear. He makes wide eyes at the back of her head, at the same time fascinated and fearful. Eventually, he drums up enough courage to begin a conversation. "That's a small bag you've packed."

Susman doesn't turn to look at him. "I'm not planning on staying very long."

Her curtness does not deter Khaya. "It's not big enough for a ... shotgun."

"Khaya," barks De Villiers, frowning into the rear-view mirror. "Shut the hell up, will you?"

"I only use my twelve gauge to scare off unwelcome visitors," says Susman. "I have other guns for other purposes." She pats the bag she insisted on keeping on her lap. It feels strange to be in the car with the men. Just a couple of hours ago she had her hands wrapped around a shotgun, and now she's hurtling in a metal contraption towards the city that poisons her dreams.

"I'm very interested in your career," ventures Khaya. "I'd love to hear about it."

"Sure," says Susman. "Let's do coffee sometime."

Khaya leans forward in his seat. "Seriously?"

"No."

The sergeant sits back and stares out of the window again.

"You've looked through the file?" De Villiers asks Susman.

"Yes."

"Questions?"

"Why did you wait until now to investigate? Sandra Longman, the first vic, was taken over three weeks ago."

"It wasn't our case until now. We don't go around chasing rich white women if it looks like they packed their own bags. They concluded she had run away. Baby blues or something."

"If you mean post-partum depression—"

"Yes, that."

"Post-what-what?" asks Khaya, but they ignore him.

"Was there any evidence of that?" asks Susman.

"No, but it may have gone undiagnosed. Untreated. But then the second woman went missing."

"Desiree van Zyl," says Robin.

"Yes."

"It's important to use their names. I mean, if you want to get a real feeling for the case. If you were able to get a real feeling for Sandra Longman, you would have known she was not depressed. You could have followed the trail sooner. And if not with Sandra, then certainly Desiree."

"Yes," De Villiers says. "But you know what it's like. The caseloads we have. If I had one case at a time, I'd be the best *fokken* detective this side of the equator."

"Okay," says Susman. "So we know that he has a 'type'. Slim, pretty brunettes. Medium height."

"With babies," chips in Khaya from the back.

Susman nods. "With babies."

"Single," adds De Villiers.

"Have you checked online dating?" Susman asks.

"I'll ask Swanepoel. Definitely worth a look."

"And what about the fathers? Ex-partners? Where are they?"

"That's the first thing we checked," says Khaya. "Sandra's boyfriend lives in the UK, the other one—Emily's ex-husband—is around. They were going through a nasty divorce, a custody battle. He has Benjamin now."

"So, his wife disappears, and he gets what he wants?"

"He's also the main beneficiary of her will. It's out-of-date. I think she meant to change it, but then the baby came."

"I'd like to question him," says Susman.

Khaya nods. "I'll set it up."

"What about the other one?" asks De Villiers.

Khaya looks at him. "Hey?"

"The other father. Desiree's baby's father."

"Anonymous sperm donor," says Khaya.

"One-night stand?" asks Susman.

Khaya laughs. "No, a real anonymous sperm donor. At a fertility clinic. She had the baby on her own."

"Let's find out who that donor is."

"It won't be easy," says De Villiers.

Susman drums her fingers on her suitcase. "I'm not expecting any part of this investigation to be easy."

They travel in silence for a while. They don't appreciate the scenery; they see blood in place of soil.

"So," says Robin. "Now we wait for the bodies to show up."

Khaya straightens up. "How do you know? He might bury them in his backyard or something. Keep them in his basement."

Susman turns to him. "This man doesn't respect these women. Not in life, not in death. He won't bury them or cremate them. He'll take what he wants and dump the rest. Rubbish dumps. Mine dumps. Rivers. They're out there. We just need to find them."

De Villiers' phone vibrates.

"Must I answer for you, Sir?"

"Who is it?" asks Devil. "The station?"

Khaya looks at the caller ID. "Er ... It's your wife. I mean, your ex-wife. Sorry."

Susman shoots the detective a questioning look.

"Must I answer?"

Before De Villiers can reply, the phone stops ringing.

"Sorry, De Villiers," says Susman. "I didn't know. About you and Anna-Mart."

"It's not official," he says, as if there is still hope. Robin's about to say something else, but De Villiers cuts her off. "About the case. We don't have much time."

Susman nods and drags her eyes off the detective to focus on the road. "What do we know about the perpetrator?"

"At this point, it's just guesswork. Probably male, probably white, between twenty and forty years old."

"Yes."

"Most likely a medium-high IQ but probably underperformed academically."

"What else?"

"Unstable home and family life. May have been institutionalised at some point."

"And mommy issues," chips in Khaya. "Serious mommy issues."

"Good," says Susman.

"Maybe he is trying to kidnap his mother, if you know what I mean. Trying to get her back—"

"Or control her," says De Villiers.

"Or kill her," says Susman. "Maybe he did kill his mother and is trying to re-enact it. Or maybe he wasn't able to kill her for whatever reason, so he is killing her through these women."

"Sjoe," says Khaya. "I will be a better father. From today."

De Villiers' eyes crinkle in the mirror. "You can start by changing a nappy every now and then."

"I will. I'm not joking."

"Rose can thank me later."

"Ha," Khaya says, smiling. "I will tell her."

"In the meantime, get Breytenbach to search the rolls of all possible institutions in our timeframe. Someone born between 1970 and 1990. We can go wider if we need to."

"And social services," adds Susman. "Any reported incident, whether or not it was found to be legitimate. Maybe it fell through the cracks."

De Villiers' phone rings again, and he curses under his breath.

"It's the station," says Khaya.

This time, Devil doesn't hesitate. "Answer it."

Khaya strains to hear; his body language becomes animated. "What? Serious?" He taps the shoulder of the detective's carseat. "Where? Okay, we're on our way."

"Looks like you've got your wish," De Villiers says to Susman. "It sounds like they've found a body."

"Funny," replies Susman. She's not smiling.

"A dead body? Funny?"

"Funny how you think a dead body is my wish. Like I have some macabre fairy godmother hanging around, granting grisly wishes."

"I wouldn't mind a fairy godmother," says Devil. "Grisly or not."

9

DEAD ANIMAL

JENNIFER WALKER'S ILLOVO FLAT, **Johannesburg, 13th of July 2014, 15:39.**

Jennifer Walker's voice is husky as she rolls off Swanepoel.

"You've made me late for my assignment," she teases. "Again."

Swanepoel grins. "Most women don't complain about my ... prowess."

The journalist laughs. "Prowess?"

"Well, what would you call it?"

She extricates herself from the twisted bed sheets and pulls on her underwear.

"Don't try to get me to talk dirty. I only do that on the third date."

"Date?" says Swanepoel. "So are we dating now?"

Jennifer throws his shirt at him, and he catches it.

"Yes," she says. "In your dreams."

He hangs his head and mutters. "Cruel."

"What's that?"

The lieutenant dresses and straps on his holstered Beretta. "I said, you're a cruel woman."

Walker runs her tongue over her sharp incisors. "You like it."

He growls. "Damn right, I like it." He reaches for her, runs his hands over her body, kisses her shapely neck. They're interrupted by a tinny rendition of an Eminem track. Swanepoel reluctantly lets go of her and grabs his ringing phone.

"Shit. It's the station. I've got three missed calls. They've realised my lunch break has gone on a little longer than usual."

"Damn that *prowess* of yours," teases Walker. She puts her hand on her jutting hip. "Well, are you going to answer?"

He casts a last lingering look at her fine body, then taps his screen. "Hello?"

"Swanepoel," says De Villiers. "Where the hell are you?"

"I ... er ..." his eyes travel to the cheap clock on the wall — a kitsch knockoff of a Swiss railway clock.

"I called the station, and they said you were out. You weren't picking up at your desk. You weren't picking up your mobile."

"I'm just—"

"Never mind, just get to Roodeplaat now."

"Okay." He fumbles with his silver watch. "I can be there in an hour."

"Make it forty minutes."

"What's the rush?"

"We've got a body. Looks like the first missing woman—Longman—but it's difficult to tell because it's—"

The line crackles.

"De Villiers?"

"Just get here," says the detective. "You'll see."

Swanepoel snatches his keys from the table. "I'm leaving right now."

When he looks up, Jennifer Walker is standing in his way. "Not so fast, lieutenant."

"I seriously have to go." Swanepoel runs his hand through his hair.

"There's been a development," she says. "What is it?"

"It's nothing."

"It doesn't look like nothing."

"I'll call you later," he says. "Maybe."

He tries to get past her, but she blocks him. "I want to know now."

He pecks her on the forehead. "Bye, Sweet Lips."

"Bastard," Jennifer mutters. "You can be a real bastard, you know that?"

"Yep," he says, not bothering to close the door on his way out. "And you like it."

She throws her high heel at his retreating figure, but he's too fast for her. The stiletto bounces off the wall in the passage, leaving a small scuff mark on the already chipped paint, and lands in the middle of the beige carpet. Walker can't help but think it looks like a dead animal.

10

HOPE IS A FLAME

ROODEPLAAT DAM, **Tshwane, 13th of July 2014, 16:12.**

The dam is unexpectedly beautiful. The water is usually being churned up by regattas, but today De Villiers notices the eerie calm of the surface, in total contrast to the buzzing forensic team setting up crime scene tape and marking prints and muddied litter with numbered flags.

"De Villiers!" exclaims a woman wearing protective gear. She pulls off her mask, revealing an attractive smile. "You look terrible!"

"Wow, Msibi," replies the detective. "So great with the compliments, as usual."

"Seriously, you look like shit. What's going on in your life? Is it really as bad as you look?"

De Villiers rubs his forehead. "You don't want to know."

"You're right." She turns to Khaya. "Who's the newbie?"

"This is Khaya," he mutters. "He's shadowing me on this case."

"Hello, Sergeant Khaya. What horrible thing did you do in your previous life that God has punished you so?"

Khaya frowns. "Excuse me?"

"To have to work for this ape," she says, rolling her thumb at De Villiers.

Khaya laughs uncomfortably.

De Villiers' eyes are daggers. "Watch it, sergeant."

Khaya stops laughing.

Msibi turns back to De Villiers and lowers her voice. "When are we going for a beer again?"

The detective looks at her, searching her eyes for a glint of humour, but she's serious. "Soon?"

"Good," says Msibi. "I don't like it that the only time we see each other is over a dead body."

"A beer will be good."

Msibi puts her hands on her hips. "Excellent. Now let's get down to the dirty."

"Hold on a minute," he says, sweeping his eyes across the scene. "Just waiting for Susman. She was right behind us. And where the hell is Swanepoel?"

"Hey?" says Msibi. "Susman's here? Detective Robin Susman?" she joins De Villiers in scanning the faces of the people on the scene.

"Ex-detective," he says. "Susman is consulting for us on this case."

Msibi looks stunned.

"I know," says De Villiers. "I didn't see it coming either."

"Major's orders," explains Khaya.

"Well, I'll be damned," Msibi says. "You feel that chill in the air? I think hell just froze over. This case seems to get more and more interesting."

Susman pops up in the distance and does a slow jog to join them.

"Robin!" shouts Msibi.

Susman smiles. "Xoliswa! Long time."

The women hug like sisters.

"Didn't think I'd see the day."

"Me, neither." Susman is slightly breathless. "But don't get used to it. I'm out of here the second we have something on this guy."

"Well, it's good to see you. I like what you've done with your..." Msibi gesticulates above her head. "Your what-what. Whatever you call that."

Susman is incredulous. "My hair?"

"Yes," says Msibi. "Your hair. You look like a ... a lion, or something. Feral. Fierce."

Before Susman has a chance to respond, De Villiers cuts in. "Have we identified the body yet?"

Msibi nods. "Good news for us, bad news for Sandra Longman's family."

"So you were right," says Khaya.

"I'm always right," says Susman. "It's a curse, really."

"When the station called," says the detective, "they said something about the body was ... unusual?"

"Well, it's more body parts, than a body. Maybe that's what they meant."

Susman's ears prick up. "Parts? All of them?"

"All but one," says Msibi.

"If he isn't scattering them, then why cut it up?" asks Khaya. "It's a lot of unnecessary work."

"Maybe the whole body was too heavy to move. Or maybe—"

"Cannibalism?" suggests Susman. "Is the missing part in this guy's fridge?"

Khaya closes his eyes. "*Ag* no, man. S*ies*."

"I thought of cannibalism, but the body isn't cut up in that way. It's not like, let's say, the fillet has been removed. The loin. It's more clean cut. Right through. Like pruning a tree. You understand what I'm saying."

Susman winces. "Which part is missing?"

"The upper thoracic. Top half of the torso."

"The breasts," says Robin. "But it's not sexual."

"He cut off her breasts?" asks Khaya.

"No, it's the whole chest and back."

"It makes sense," says Susman. "What signifies a mother more than lactating breasts?"

"But what's he ... doing with it?"

"That's for us to find out," says De Villiers. "Let's see what he's left us, shall we?"

Msibi's expression darkens. "I hope you didn't eat lunch."

They walk over to the sheet lying on the ground in the stretched shade of a willow tree. Msibi gestures to the person closest to the cloth to remove it.

Bile rises in Robin's throat. She chokes and looks away, blocking her flaring nostrils with her hand.

"As you can see," says Msibi, "the parts have been cleanly severed. Look at this shoulder joint—cut clean through—and this abdomen. I mean, you can see that it's been in the water, but—"

"How did he get such a smooth surface?" asks De Villiers. "Butcher saw?"

Susman is trying to swallow the vomit simmering in her throat. "He froze it."

Msibi moves towards Susman and holds her elbow. "Robin, are you okay?"

"I'm okay," she says. If she can just breathe, she'll avoid the panic attack.

"You're white," says Khaya. "Like, seriously white."

Robin is suddenly irritated. "Do you think this is the first dead body I've seen?"

Khaya stammers, but nothing comes out. Perhaps he's remembering the shotgun.

Devil motions to a nearby bank. "Maybe we should all ... let's go sit down."

"I just need a minute." Susman walks away and sits under a tree.

Msibi hisses at them through clenched teeth. "What were you guys thinking?"

De Villiers looks sorry. He casts his eyes down at the muddy grass. "Denton insisted."

"And did the major force you to bring her to see a mutilated body within hours of fetching her?" seethes Msibi. "Do you know what that woman has been through?"

"Look, she's either on this job, or she's not," says De Villiers. "I can't shield her from the violence she's going to see. We've got a case to crack. She's not a child. And I'm not a babysitter."

"Yes, genius. Correct. She's not a child. She's a woman with severe PTSD. She's not the same ball-breaking detective you used to know. If she's going to be of any help to you on this case you will have to protect her to a certain degree. You must—"

De Villiers' phone rings, slicing the tension between them. He blinks his assent at Msibi, who nods back, and then he takes the call.

"André!" exclaims Anna-Mart. "Have you heard anything from Niel?"

"No. Still not. I was wondering if you had."

Her voice is shaking. "I would have told you! Of course, I would have told you."

"Have you seen the news? Rockets being fired all day. The pictures of those poor school kids."

"Yes," says De Villiers. "I've seen the news. It's terrible. But his kibbutz is far away from the Strip."

"He's not at his kibbutz," his wife says. "The phone there just rings. And his cell phone has been dead for days."

"Maybe they ... maybe they've moved somewhere else," says De Villiers. "To be sure to be out of danger."

"André. What if he was travelling near the war zone? What if he's lying somewhere, injured? What if—"

"Anna. Stop. You'll drive yourself mad."

"Stop? How can I stop? I can't help thinking about it. How can I not think about it?"

Her meaning is clear. He may be a cold-blooded bastard, but she isn't.

"Worrying won't help," he says. "We need to stay rational."

"Rational!" she yells. "He's not even nineteen. He's still a baby!"

"He is not a baby, *lief*. Niel is a responsible, resourceful young man. He'll be fine. I'm sure we'll hear from him any day now."

Anna-Mart is quiet for a moment, and De Villiers wonders if she's crying. But then her voice comes back, closer than before. "I lie awake at night."

De Villiers exhales silently and looks at the sky, which is turning a warm pink. It's scratched over with cirrus clouds.

She sniffs. "I lie there, and it's like I can hear the bombs going off. I can hear the whistling of the rockets."

"If there was bad news—" begins De Villiers.

"No news is good news, I know. But Niel could be buried under debris. He could be a ... what do you call them? John Doe."

Khaya approaches looking grim. "We need you," he mouths.

De Villiers nods.

"Are you there?" asks his wife.

"I need to go. We're at a—"

"Oh."

"Anna. I know that ... I know that our lawyers have recommended we don't speak to each other while the proceedings are underway."

"I don't care about that."

"Maybe we can see each other?" he says. "Talk more. About Niel."

"Okay."

"Devil," calls Msibi. He nods at her.

"So, you'll see me?" De Villiers asks Anna-Mart.

"You're the only one," she says, but stops.

His voice is gruff. "I'm here."

"You're the only one who can talk me down. I shouldn't be saying this, André, but—"

Hope is a flame in his chest. "But?"

"Ah, nothing. You need to go. We'll talk tonight."

11

HUMMING IN BLOOD

SWANEPOEL IS GUNNING his Mazda towards Roodeplaat Dam, Metallica rattling the windows. The music fades as a call comes through the Bluetooth speaker.

"I'm almost there!" he yells. "Five minutes. Maybe ten."

"Mr Swanepoel?" says a gentle female voice, mature and maternal.

"Hey? Who's there?"

"Mr Swanepoel, it's Boitumelo Gingaba."

"Who?"

"Sister Boitumelo, from the Holy Cross."

Swanepoel eases his foot off the accelerator. "Is my mother okay?"

"Mrs Swanepoel has taken a turn."

"What do you mean, a turn? What does that mean?"

The bass of the previous song is still humming in his blood.

"She ... had a reaction, to the latest treatment."

He's at a loss for words.

"Mr Swanepoel?" says the nurse.

"Is she okay?"

"I think it would be best to come in."

If he didn't show up at the dam, De Villiers would kill him. "I'm late for an urgent meeting. I'll come straight afterwards."

"To be clear, I'd recommend you come in right away."

"Shit," he says, and brakes hard.

"Excuse me?"

"Sorry." He looks for oncoming traffic. "I'm turning around. I'll be there as soon as I can."

~

Parkview Police Station 13th of July 2014, 18:48.

Khaya spins his office chair to face De Villiers, who is behind his desk, searching a document and frowning as if his life depends on it.

"Msibi's just emailed her top-line autopsy report," he says.

De Villiers looks up at him, light in his eyes despite the time of day. "That was quick. She's efficient, that Msibi. She may drink too much *Zamalek* and cheat at poker, but she's worth having around."

Susman, sitting in the other chair, pipes up. "She was always my favourite Forensic."

Khaya is relieved to see that colour has returned to Susman's cheeks. "Msibi said she'll send the comprehensive file soon, but there are a few things she picked up already that might help us."

"Good woman," says De Villiers.

A rough-looking lieutenant Swanepoel finally walks into the office and throws his car keys on his desk.

"Swanepoel!" says De Villiers. "Where the bloody hell have you been?"

"Just lay off, Devil," Swanepoel says. "It's been a tough day."

De Villiers blinks in disbelief. "*You've* had a tough day? Really?"

"Yes," says Swanepoel. "Really."

"You've been MIA the whole day doing God-knows-what while we've been looking at body parts."

The lieutenant doesn't apologise. "I'm here now."

"Well," says De Villiers, his face creasing in a fake smile. "Aren't we the lucky ones?"

"Did you say *body parts?*"

"Forensics identified her as the first victim kidnapped."

"Longman?" asks Swanepoel.

They nod.

"Shit."

Khaya looks at him. "What?"

Swanepoel shakes his head. "Nothing. I just ... I'm the one who interviewed her family. They were so hopeful that she'd be okay."

"Miracles never cease," says De Villiers.

"What do you mean?"

"You have a heart, Swanepoel. What can I say? I'm shocked."

Khaya, for once, is less forgiving. "Breytenbach had to break the news to them. To the family. You weren't here."

Susman rotates her chair so that Swanepoel can see her. "Well, let's get on with it. We've got a lot to do."

The lieutenant freezes. "Holy shit, Susman? Is that you? You look completely ... different. I hardly recognised you."

"It's me. Have I aged that much in a couple of years?"

"That's not what I meant. Maybe it's just that—"

Susman taps her shoe against the leg of the desk while she waits for him to answer.

"Maybe it's just that I thought I'd never see you again."

"Can we get back to the case at hand?" asks De Villiers, looking at his watch. "I need to get out of here soon."

"You have somewhere better to be?" asks Swanepoel. "That's a first."

Susman shuffles the papers on her lap. "Any evidence was likely washed away by the water."

"I thought as much," says De Villiers.

"But they found something."

They all look at her expectantly. "We're listening."

"Sawdust," she says. "At least, they think it's sawdust. Trace amounts wedged into the open flesh."

Swanepoel frowns. "Is that even possible?"

"Are you questioning Msibi?"

"Nope," Swanepoel shakes his head. "Never."

"So, in other words," says Khaya, "the killer used some kind of wood saw."

"A jigsaw," says Swanepoel.

"Hey?"

"It's called a jigsaw," repeats Swanepoel.

"Like the puzzles?"

"The puzzles are named after the saw, not the other way around."

"What kind of sawdust?" asks De Villiers. "I mean, what kind of wood?"

"S.A. Pine."

Swanepoel snorts. "As common as dog shit."

"That's a charming turn of phrase," says Susman, and Swanepoel shrugs as if the idea of charm had never occurred to him.

De Villiers stands up. "So our perp works with timber. He's possibly a carpenter, or his hobby is woodwork or furniture making. Or he works at some kind of a timber store..."

"And I was right," says Susman. "About him freezing the body before sawing it. The remains have signs of frostbite."

Khaya shudders. "Freezing the body ... to store it? To keep it fresh?"

"To get that precise, clean cut," says Susman. "You wouldn't be able to achieve that with a fresh body."

They all look at her, slightly horrified.

After a while, Swanepoel breaks the tension. "Funny, hey, Susman?"

"What's that?"

"Funny how yesterday you were probably milking cows and today you're talking about a fresh body. Like you've never left the force."

"*Ja*, well," sighs Susman. "Somebody had to come show you guys how to crack a case."

"Haha," he says, without laughing.

De Villiers clicks his pen closed and grabs his jacket. "Okay, people, that's enough. It's seven o'clock. Let's call it a night."

Khaya frowns at him. "But, sir, we're ... nowhere. Two women are missing who might still be alive."

The guilt De Villiers feels makes his jaws ache. "I need to be somewhere. And Susman needs a lift to her hotel. Her day has been long enough."

"I don't mind working for a few more hours," she says. "Chase some leads."

"I can also stay," says Swanepoel.

"No," says De Villiers, and they all look at him as if he's spoken in tongues.

"No?"

De Villiers leaves his desk. "Strict orders from the major."

An amused smile plays on Susman's face. She turns away from him, back to the file. "Since when do I listen to orders from the major?"

"Not *your* orders," De Villiers says. "Mine. I'm not to leave your side unless there is a guard on duty. He's waiting outside your hotel room as we speak."

"A guard? Why?"

"Better safe than sorry. Also, I was supposed to have you there by six."

Susman whips around, annoyed. "So I get a guard AND a curfew?"

"He's just trying to look after you."

"If the major knows anything," says Susman. "It's that I can look after myself."

12

MERCURIAL

DETECTIVE DE VILLIERS brakes smoothly in the drop-off zone of the hotel and leaves the engine running. "Here we are. Can I walk you up? Carry your ... bag?"

Susman wrenches the passenger door open and climbs out. "No, it's not necessary."

"Sure?"

"Yes, Devil. Thanks for the lift."

"I'll pick you up at eight tomorrow morning?"

"I'll be up at five."

"In that case, I'll see you at six. Here's your room keycard. And a phone."

Robin enters the building and strides towards the elevator. At the door to her hotel room, she greets the guard.

"Ma'am," says the uniformed man. She's already unlocked the door, so his warning comes too late. A rush of anxiety tears through her when she sees there's someone in her room.

"Robin, darling!" says Clementine. "You're an hour late!"

Susman breathes out slowly, trying to keep her pulse under control. "Holy shit, Clem," she whispers. "You almost gave me a heart attack."

Clementine's grin melts away into an expression of pure mortification. "Oh God, I'm sorry!"

Susman drops her bag where she stands. She didn't realise how exhausted she was.

"I sent a message to the station."

"I didn't get it."

"I can tell by the look on your face! Martini?" Clementine holds up the bullet-shaped steel cocktail shaker.

Susman doesn't move.

"I'm sorry I startled you! I wasn't thinking! Come here. I want a big hug."

They meet in the middle of the room and hug.

"Look at you," says Clem, a hint of tears in her eyes which she quickly blinks away. "You look wonderful."

"That I doubt very much."

"You do. You've ... grown your hair. It's lovely."

"Not on purpose," says Susman. "There are not many hairdressers in Rosendal."

"Well, you look as pretty as a picture." She pours them both a generous Martini and pops two olives in each. "Here, take this. Let's drink to seeing each other again."

They chink glasses and take a sip. The drink is cold, but the gin warms Robin's throat. "You've always known how to pour an excellent Martini."

Clementine smiles. "It's one of my—very many—talents."

"Maybe the gin will stop my heart from beating right out of my chest."

"Oh God," chuckles Clementine. "No more unintended surprises, I swear! But I am so happy to see you. I can't believe you're here. It's marvellous."

"How did you know?"

"How do you think? I had to drag it out of Alistair. He forbade me from pestering you. I'm not supposed to be here, so don't you dare tell him!"

"I haven't even seen him yet."

Clementine shoots Susman a puzzled look. "Really? How odd. I thought he'd rush to welcome you."

"More like, avoid me at all costs." Susman takes a large sip of her drink.

"Nonsense," says Clementine. "He's so grateful to have you here—"

"He didn't leave me much choice."

"He sent flowers." Clementine gestures at an explosion of petals in the corner. Tulips.

"Oh."

"Not that you could miss them!" she chuckles. "Probably because he feels horrible about making you come out here."

Robin smirks. "You read the card, then?"

"Of course I did! I had to make sure you weren't keeping a secret lover or something like that."

"Really, Clem?" Susman chuckles. "A secret lover?"

"A farmer from the Free State who couldn't stand the thought of having one night without you."

"So it disappointed you, then, seeing that it was from—"

"—my dim-witted brother, yes."

"Alistair is anything but a dimwit. He's the best major the station has ever had."

"Dim-witted enough to let you go."

"Yes, well. I didn't give him much choice."

"You're both dim-witted, then. Let's have another drink."

Clementine tops up their Martinis and opens a box of fresh croissants. "You're perfect for each other, you both know that."

"No, we're not. Not anymore."

"Damn it, Robin!" exclaims Clementine in mock frustration. "How are we ever supposed to be real sisters if you two won't bloody co-operate?"

"We are real sisters, Clem," says Robin, and lifts her glass. "The same Martini runs in our veins." The women exchange an affectionate look. "Besides," Susman peels a crust off her croissant and pops it into her mouth. "Even if I wanted to move back—which I don't—and even if I wanted to be with Alistair again ... it would be too late, wouldn't it? What is his wife like, by the way?"

"*Pshh!*" says Clementine. "Comparing the two of you is like comparing merlot to dishwater."

"That's a bit harsh! Wait, who is the dishwater?"

"She is! Truly, darling. She's pretty and athletic and platinum blonde..."

"Sounds like a terrible wife to have," mutters Robin.

"Clearly fertile, and frightfully clever—"

"Poor Alistair!" says Susman. "To be stuck with someone like that!"

"But she is as dull as anything."

"Ah, Clem. I'm sure she's not."

"Watching paint dry, darling. Conversations with her are like watching paint dry. Attractive paint, nicely packaged, but paint nonetheless. I avoid it at all costs."

"You're being especially mean," says Susman, looking into her empty glass and sighing. "You're a good friend."

"I'd literally rather look after all three of my kids for a whole day—okay, maybe a whole afternoon—than talk to her for 10 minutes."

Susman chuckles. "You wouldn't."

"Okay, you're right, I'm exaggerating. But now you know."

"Know what? That you're a good liar?"

"Now you know why Alistair gaped at me for so long during his wedding ceremony."

Robin stops laughing. "Why?"

"He was thinking about you. He's always thinking about you."

"Nonsense." Susman flicks a piece of flint off her jeans.

"I don't blame him, of course. I was a little in love with you, myself."

Robin pretends to be offended. "Was? Past tense? What about now?"

"Still head over heels. But you know..."

"Yes?"

Clementine's eyes glitter. "You're gorgeous, darling. Mercurial. But you are not an easy woman to love."

13

COLD

De Villiers sits across from his wife, their body language equally stiff. The house feels at the same time so familiar, yet so different. The scent of home; the feel of the smooth wooden armrest beneath his palms; the shadow the ceiling light casts on the walls.

"I tried to reach out to you," says Anna-Mart. "Over and over again."

De Villiers looks down at his hands. His wedding ring tan has almost disappeared. "We shouldn't be having this conversation. The attorneys—"

"Of course we should!"

"It's too late." He thinks it might be true.

"Why? Because we've filed the papers? I don't care about the bloody papers! I don't care about anything but you and Niel!"

De Villiers searches Anna-Mart's face. "If being with me was so lonely, why are you willing to do it again?"

"Because I love you, André! I miss you. What we had was good."

"Not good enough," he says.

"How can you be so cold?"

"Cold?" De Villiers bristles. "I wasn't the one who filed for divorce."

"Do you have any idea how difficult it is ... was ... being married to you? It's like, even when you're here, you're not really here. Your head is back at the station, or the crime scene, or some other dark place."

"I know. I'm sorry. I'm hardly husband material. Never have been."

She shakes her head sadly. "That's not true."

"It is," he says, pain etched in his face. He could murder a double brandy and Coke, but wants to have a clear head for this conversation.

"We could try again," Anna-Mart says.

A part of De Villiers is joyous at hearing this. He wants Anna-Mart; wants life to go back to normal. But sitting across from her now, watching her hopeful face, the joy leaks away. The tragic truth is that she'd be happier without him. Happier with someone else who could give her the emotional intimacy she craves. His sinuses burn with tears. "No," he mutters.

Anna-Mart stares at him, then sits forward, face buried in her palms, and weeps. The detective's phone rings and Devil reaches for it.

"Leave it!" she shouts. "For God's sake!"

"I can't," he says. "It's an international number. Israel! Hello? Hello? Niel?" Static whooshes down the line.

"Niel?" asks Anna-Mart, wiping her tears on the back of her hand.

De Villiers taps the icon for speakerphone. "Hello? Niel?"

The fizzing sound fills the room, and De Villiers and Anna-Mart lock desperate eyes. The line goes dead.

"Damn it!" he yells.

"It could have been him," whispers Anna-Mart.

"It could have been anyone," replies De Villiers.

14

TAKEN

EMERGENCY CALL CENTRE **14th of July 2014, 5:04.**

The emergency call centre is chaotic with incoming calls. Anything less would be unusual. A mature woman wearing jeans and a *Cure* T-shirt has almost finished her shift. She arches her spine, stretches her arms above her, and rocks in her seat. She clicks the flashing button which she hopes will be her last call. It's been a long graveyard shift; she has cats to feed, and her bed is calling her.

"Emergency Assist," she says, loud and clear. "How can I help you?"

"It's my sister," replies the caller.

There's a dog-eared poster on the wall. *Do YOU need to talk to someone?*

"Your sister? Is this a medical emergency?"

"No," says the caller. "I need the police."

"The police, ma'am? What is your emergency?"

"My sister is missing."

"Your sister is missing? How long has she been missing?"

The caller's voice is high and anxious. "I don't know. Overnight?"

"I'm here to help you. Try to keep calm."

"You don't understand. She's gone. We were supposed to meet. She wasn't answering her phone and ... she left her baby here. It's like that other woman. Those other women. I don't know what to do."

"Which other women?"

"Those other three women ... who were..." she cries. "They found a body yesterday."

"Ma'am, what is your sister's address? I'll dispatch someone immediately."

"Oh my God, she's been taken," says the distraught woman. "She's been taken."

15

HANDS CURL INTO FISTS

PARKVIEW POLICE STATION, **14th of July 2014, 8:48.**

It's early, but sweat is already blooming under Swanepoel's arms. De Villiers catches him as he walks past the coffee station. "You okay?"

"Since when do you care?"

"I care," says De Villiers.

"That's what I like about you, Devil."

De Villiers shoots him a questioning look.

Swanepoel smirks. "You're full of bloody surprises."

"Hey," calls Breytenbach from the other side of the open-plan office. They both look at him. "They're talking about our guy again."

"What now?"

"The news," says Breytenbach, grabbing the remote and increasing the volume. Jennifer Walker's holding a microphone. Her lips are painted red.

"Since when do we care what a journalist has to say?" asks Swanepoel, but his voice is drowned out by the television.

"—and that's when you realised that something was wrong?" Walker asks.

"Yes," says the woman she is interviewing.

"Because your sister, Denise Metlerkamp, used to check in with you every night before going to bed. And last night—"

"She didn't."

"Why would you do this?" asks Walker. "This 'checking in'?"

"To make sure we were both okay."

"You were close?"

"*Are* close. We *are* close."

"Of course," says the journalist, and moves to face the camera squarely. "If you have any information regarding the disappearance of Denise Metlerkamp—" A picture of the missing woman flashes up on the screen, captioned with the Parkview Police Station's contact number. "Please call the authorities. If you have seen Denise Metlerkamp, or Desiree van Zyl, or Emily Shuter—these are their photos—please call in. Any information could help."

"At least she gave out our number, not her own," says Swanepoel.

Breytenbach laughs.

"Before I sign off: a warning. If you fit this profile, please be cautious. If you are a single mother with a young infant, medium height, brunette, living in Gauteng—if you fit this profile please consider yourself a possible target."

De Villiers rolls his eyes. "And ... here comes the hysteria."

Susman stops examining the file in her hand. "I'd rather have hysterical women being cautious than—"

The detective shakes his head. "You're right. But it will make our jobs more difficult. I don't have the human resources to field calls from every bloody brunette in the city."

As if on cue, all the phones in the office start ringing.

"Here we go," says Breytenbach.

Susman flinches as someone touches her shoulder. She spins around, and instinctively her hands curl into fists.

Major Alistair Denton looks awkward. "Apologies," he mutters. "I didn't mean to—"

"Hello, Alistair," says Robin.

"Would you mind coming to my office for a moment?"

"I'm right in the middle of something," she says.

The major doesn't back down. "I realise you're very busy." The cops standing around them pretend they're not listening. "But I just need a moment."

"Okay," Susman says. She passes the papers to Khaya. "Finish going through these credit card statements, will you? You're looking for any overlap between the four women."

"Yes, ma'am."

"Gym memberships, medical aid, restaurants, anything. Any link at all."

"Got it."

Once they step inside Major Denton's office, he closes the door softly behind them, muting the station's ambience. He offers her a chair.

"I'd rather stand," she says, arms crossed.

"Robin. I have some intel. I think it would be better if you were to sit."

"Is that her?" asks Susman.

"Excuse me?"

"That picture, on your desk. Is that your ... wife?"

"Oh," Alastair says, glancing over at the frame. "Yes. That's Katherine."

"And the baby?"

He pauses and touches the top of his right ear the way he always does. "Yes. Samuel."

"Congratulations."

Alastair takes a breath. "Thank you. And thank you for coming through for this case. I know it must be very ... difficult."

"You sent tulips. To my hotel room."

"I know they're your favourite."

"They used to be my favourite. It was a different time. Things change."

"I'm sorry," the major says.

"Me too."

Their eyes meet, but the resulting wave of emotion is too difficult to endure. They both look away.

Alastair walks around his desk and sits down. "I have to tell you about a development."

Susman turns her body to face him. "About the Turbine Hall Gang? Early parole?"

Alastair's surprised. "Yes. How did you know?"

"I was your best detective for a reason."

"Many reasons," he says, pausing for effect. "I just want you to know that nothing is going to happen to you."

"I think we both know it's too late for that."

He winces. "Nothing will happen to you this time."

"I wondered why I had a bodyguard," muses Susman. "Now it makes sense."

"You'll be under protection for as long as you need it. Also, I don't want you going out in the field for this case. It's not essential. You can consult from here."

"Of course it's essential!"

"I don't want you exposed to any more violence than is strictly necessary."

"You shouldn't have brought me out here if you didn't want me looking at dead bodies."

"I know. God help me, I know. I just ... I just think of those poor women. Those babies. I can't stand it. I knew you wouldn't be able to stand it either."

Susman's mouth is a hard line as she walks to the door and wrenches it open. "Damn you." She freezes in the doorway, her back to him. "Damn you for thinking of me when you heard about this case."

The major holds up a hand, wordlessly asking her to wait. She doesn't.

"Damn you for thinking about me at all."

She makes her way back to the open-plan office. The whole police station is ringing off the hook.

"Susman!" exclaims De Villiers.

Her anger is pulsing in every cell. "What?"

"We got an anonymous call. Claimed he found vic two. Van Zyl. Desiree."

"Not alive?"

"Very much ... dead."

"Parts, again?" Susman asks.

"Yes."

"Well, then. If it's her," she says, "It's official. I won't be sleeping until we find this guy."

"Sorry," says De Villiers. His own face is hardly well-rested.

"It's okay. To be honest, I wasn't sleeping much before this case, anyway."

Devil gives her a skew smile in solidarity, then swipes his keys off his untidy desk. He whistles sharply to get Khaya's attention.

Susman uncrosses her arms. "Where are we going?"

"To Hyde Park. To look at the body."

"Let's go," she says.

De Villiers looks uncomfortable; mumbles something that sounds like *No*.

"I'm coming along, De Villiers. You can wipe that awkward look off your face."

"Don't take this the wrong way," he says. "My orders are to keep you out of the gruesome stuff."

Susman sneers at him. "That's bullshit, and you know it."

"I know!" he says, "I know. But ... it's complicated. Your ... history—"

"Devil," Susman says, grinding her teeth. "Do you want me on this case, or not?"

He hesitates. "I didn't, at first."

"You decide right now if you want me here or not. I don't do half-jobs.

Believe me, no one would be happier than me to go home right now. So just say the word, and I'm gone."

Khaya glances around, perhaps looking for popcorn.

"I want you here, Susman. I want you on the case."

"Good." She snatches the car keys out of De Villiers' hand. "I'll drive."

RE-MEMBERING MOTHER

DE VILLIERS SWITCHES the car radio station from indie rock to the news.

"At dawn today," reads the speaker in a neutral, clipped accent, "two Hamas cells from the Gaza Strip infiltrated southern Israel through secret underground tunnels. They emerged near Kibbutz NirAm, a residential community who have been living in terror not only of the rocket fire that rattles their window frames but kidnappings from underground. Peace talks—"

He turns the volume down.

"I preferred the music," says Susman, flying through a green light and then getting stuck behind a taxi that has stopped in the middle of the road.

"Me, too," says De Villiers. "But my son—"

"God! Niel? The last time I saw him, he must have been fourteen!"

"Probably."

"Turn right here," directs Khaya from the back seat. "At this robot."

Susman indicates to turn. "And now?" asks Susman. "Finished school?"

"Yes. He got his colours for cricket. And three distinctions."

"Got his brains from his mom, then?"

Khaya laughs, a little too loudly. Devil shoots him an annoyed look.

"I'm kidding, De Villiers," says Susman. "Lighten up, will you? I know it's been a *kak* morning so far." She takes her eyes off the road, briefly, to glance at him. "What? Is something up? With Niel?"

"We can't get hold of him."

"You can't get hold of him because he's backpacking around the world and he hasn't posted on Instagram, or you can't get hold of him because something's happened?"

"We're not sure yet. Haven't heard from him since the latest spate of attacks." He looks at the car radio.

"Niel's in Israel? Holy shit. No wonder you're worried. Anna-Mart must be—"

"This is it," says Khaya. "We're here. They said we must go to the back of the centre where they keep the bins."

"He wanted us to find it, then. He wanted to dump it, but he wanted us to find it almost as soon as he had done it. He needs us to acknowledge him."

"Why?" asks De Villiers.

Susman doesn't answer. They climb out of the car and approach the cordoned-off area behind the shopping centre. Msibi is happy to see them. "Greetings, my trio. My tribe."

Susman frowns in the harsh sunlight. "Is the same body part missing this time?"

"Not even a 'hello'?" asks Msibi. "I know I'm good at my job, but I'm not an automaton, you know. I do have feelings."

"Sorry, Msibi," says Robin. "Hello. Good morning. I brought you a coffee."

"You did?"

"No, but I should have. Your report yesterday was excellent."

"Thank you," the forensic analyst says.

"I'll owe you one."

Msibi purses her lips. "I've heard that before. Okay, so, in my opinion, definitely the same guy. Same M.O."

Khaya interjects. "So it *is* the same body part that is missing?"

"*Sjoe*, whippersnapper. I'm getting there. Didn't your mother teach you that there is nothing to be gained from rushing a woman?"

"Sorry."

"I like you. You're cute. Like a little puppy."

"A ... puppy?"

"A little chocolate Labrador."

"She's messing with you, Khaya," says De Villiers.

"So," says Msibi. "Same M.O. Abducted, strangled, frozen, cut, dumped."

De Villiers looks thoughtful. "Does he keep them alive for any amount of time? Before he kills them?"

"Yes. A couple of days. Their nails are dirty, chipped. Like they've tried to escape. Tried to dig a way out, or up."

"Why does he keep them alive?" asks Khaya. "Is he lonely?"

"Maybe."

"If he keeps them for the company they are bound to shatter his illusion," says Susman. "To disappoint him, by trying to escape, or scream—"

De Villiers nods. "Something that makes him angry, by the look of the marks on their necks."

"Cutaneous bruising and abrasions, no rupture of neck muscles, fracture of the larynx and cricoid cartilage. General signs of asphyxia," says Msibi.

Susman takes a sharp breath. "To kill someone with your bare hands, face-to-face. To watch the life drain out of them. So intimate."

"He's angry," says De Villiers.

"Yes," says Susman.

"Angry with his mother?" asks Khaya.

"I'd say so, yes. Or an ex-lover. Or both. At this advanced stage, his psychosis may cause him to see every female as his mother. In his mind, every female he comes across now is deserving of punishment."

Msibi gestures at a nearby wheelie bin that is being swept for evidence. "This is the bin we found the body in."

"Any idea who called it in?"

"No," says Khaya. "They said at the station that it was probably some kind of gleaner."

The detective frowns. "Gleaner?"

"Like those guys with their big trolleys who collect stuff to recycle. Or someone homeless, looking for leftover food. Maybe a foreigner without papers. It's someone who doesn't want to get involved with the police."

Msibi takes them over to where a large yellow tarpaulin is stretched out on the ground, with bricks weighing down the corners. In the middle is Desiree Van Zyl's body.

"The pelvis is missing," says Susman, past the lump in her throat. "First he took breasts, then a womb."

"There's something else," says the forensic analyst. She goes down on her haunches and points to a neat row of little holes.

"Staple holes?" asks De Villiers.

"That's what I thought," says Msibi. "So this guy has some carpentry set-up, right? And a staple gun."

"I don't understand," says Khaya, looking slightly paler than usual. "Was he torturing her?"

"No, the staple wounds are post mortem. It's more like he was—"

"Practising," says Susman.

Msibi nods. "It's like he sees the bodies as ... material."

"He's joining them?" asks De Villiers. "The parts?"

Susman nods. "I'm guessing that he's seeking women, mothers, who look like his mother, and taking from them the part that he recognises. He's starting with the core and building outwards."

"He's building his mother," says De Villiers. Sweat beads his forehead.

"Yes. He is ... remembering her. As in, dismembering these women, to re-member his mother. Creating a composite of her."

"But why?" asks Devil. "Why re-create the person you hate so much?"

"Parental bonds are very ... complicated. You can despise a parent but at the same time be desperate for their love and approval. In an extreme case like this, I think she was probably abusive. She damaged him physically and emotionally, most likely from a tender age. Now he craves power over her. To see the fear in the women's eyes; he knows he has complete control. Now he is killing her repeatedly. And at the same time, trying to force her to exist again."

17

SLICE BY SLICE

THE MAN WATCHES HIS PREY. He's peeling an apple with a paring knife and eating it slice by slice. There is a stench of urine and stale sweat. The bound woman, Denise Metlerkamp, has a plan.

"What are you working on?" she asks.

"None of your business," replies the man. He's sitting on an old crate.

Despite the nauseating smell of the place, her mouth waters at the sight of the apple. She hasn't eaten in days. "I'd love to see it."

He laughs bitterly and stabs at the fruit in his hand.

"My father," says Denise. "My father used to make some furniture. He had a workshop just like this."

The man spits an apple seed on the floor, then wipes his lips with the back of his hand. "I don't care about your father."

"Sometimes he'd even make me these little pieces. Like little pieces of furniture, for my doll's house."

The man pauses, then continues to cut the apple.

"He's probably so worried right now. My dad. And my sister. My sister must be frantic. My whole family. We're close."

He ignores her.

"I wish I could just ... just see my baby again."

He looks at her incredulously. "I wouldn't count on that happening."

"His name is Christopher," says Denise. "He's the sweetest thing. You saw him when you ... when you picked me up. What do you think will happen to him?"

"Mothers abandon babies all the time."

"I didn't abandon him. I would never."

"You did," he says.

"No, I love him too much. I'm a good mother. I'd never leave him. Never. Not even for a moment."

"All mothers end up ... leaving their kids."

"That's not true. I've never been away from Christopher, not for a moment. Not in the five months since I gave birth. I can't even put him in his cot; I miss him too much. I spent months preparing his nursery. I painted it and put all these pictures up. I filled it with soft blankets and cuddly toys. It's the perfect room for a baby. Just perfect. But I can't bear to have him sleep in another room, even though it's right next to mine. So he sleeps in my bed, next to me, or on my chest. We cuddle all night, and he feeds whenever he's hungry. I am there for him all the time. I am everything to him. He won't know what to do without me."

The man has stopped eating.

"Look at me," Denise pleads. "Look at me!"

He trawls his eyes over to her.

"Look at my breasts," she says. "Look how swollen they are. Look how they are leaking, just talking about my boy. I need to be with him. I need to feed him."

"There are other ways for babies to eat," says the man. "He can have a bottle."

"A bottle? He's never had a bottle in his life! He doesn't need a bottle, he needs me! Not just now. Not just for milk. I am the one who will care for him for his whole life. *His whole life*. You won't take that away from him, will you?"

The man becomes agitated.

"Please," she says. "I'll do anything."

He stands, the knife glinting in his hand. "I think you should keep quiet now."

18

HOLY CROSS

HOLY CROSS HOSPITAL, **ICU. 14th of July 2014, 11:02.**

Swanepoel sits by his mother's side, holding her cold, slack hand. He speaks tenderly to her, just loudly enough to be heard over the incessant beeping and whirring of the hospital equipment.

"So then I thought of you, you know. How you and Dad used to take us to that river—where was it? And we would fish. And you'd make sandwiches, and they were always soggy because of the juice. Because you'd freeze our juice bottles overnight and then put them in the cooler bag with the sandwiches, and then the condensation would make them soggy. But at least the juice was cold."

The curtain is suddenly dragged across; silver rings sing on the steel pole.

"Oh! Mr Swanepoel," says the nurse. "I'm sorry. I didn't realise you were here."

"Can she hear me?"

The nurse stops bustling. "Excuse me?"

"Do you think my mother can hear me?"

"Someone is always listening."

He looks at the old woman again. "She looks so peaceful."

"It's your company that does it. She's always peaceful after your visits." Her expression of softness morphs into discomfort. "Mr Swanepoel. There is the matter—"

He's abrupt. "Yes, I know."

"A delicate matter."

"I know," says Swanepoel. "The bills."

"Esmé, in finance, asked me to send you to her once you got in. I'm terribly sorry to have to say this at such a trying time. We can always have her moved if it is causing too much strain on you, financially speaking. Your mother wouldn't want that."

Swanepoel shakes his head. "No. No. I want her here. I want her to get the best care possible. No matter what it costs."

"She's a fortunate woman," says the nurse.

"Fortunate?" asks Swanepoel. "She's dying."

"Everyone passes eventually. It's how you live, that counts. Your love surrounds your mother. Look at her. That is a look of grace."

19

COMMON DENOMINATOR

"I TOLD you I'd buy you a coffee," says Susman, as the waitress takes away their cups.

"It's the least you could do!" replies Msibi, and grins.

"Ah, Msibi. Forever gracious."

Msibi turns her attention to De Villiers. "What's that white powder you've got there in your hands? You skimming cocaine from the evidence room?"

"Ha," says Devil. "I wish."

"What is it?"

"Headache powder," he says. "Khaya swears it works."

"And what do you think?"

"I think it's better than nothing. Also, coffee helps."

"You've had headaches since we met," says Susman.

"Ah!" says De Villiers. "So you've found the common denominator."

"Haha. So what I mean is, that's a long time. Have you had it checked out?

"Of course I've had it checked out."

Breytenbach's phone rings, and he jumps to silence it.

"Properly, by a specialist?" asks Susman.

"I've had every scan that's ever been invented. The answer is always the same. Nothing there."

"Poor Devil," jokes Susman. "No brain? That's a tough diagnosis to hear."

Msibi and Khaya chuckle. De Villiers gives Robin a skew smile.

"But that's good, right?" asks Khaya. "That they have found nothing wrong?"

Susman looks serious. "Not necessarily."

Breytenbach's phone rings again. He curses under his breath and silences it.

"They say it's the job. Stress," says De Villiers.

"Maybe after this case you need to come to stay on the farm for a while," says Susman. "You can help me feed the chickens and tend the sheep. It's very therapeutic."

"Never going to happen," says De Villiers. "I'm a city boy, born and bred."

Msibi purses her lips. "Maybe that's the problem."

"The doctors say there are only two solutions to stop the migraines."

"Yes?" says Msibi.

"Quit the job, or cut off your head." He waits for them to laugh. They don't.

Susman takes a sip of her coffee. "For someone like you, that's the same thing."

De Villiers nods. "Exactly."

Breytenbach's phone chimes again, and everyone turns to stare at him.

"Aren't you going to answer that? Someone is obviously trying very hard to get hold of you."

"It's no one," he says, shoving the phone into his jacket pocket.

"It doesn't sound like 'no one'," says De Villiers.

"Someone stalking you, Breytenbach?" asks Msibi.

"What?"

"You have an ex-girlfriend who won't let you go? You want me to sort her out?"

"No," he says.

"Put it this way," says De Villiers. "If that phone rings again and you don't answer it, I will answer it for you. Either that or I'll jam it—"

"Okay, okay."

It rings again, and Breytenbach curses and takes it outside the coffee shop. De Villiers calls the waitress over and orders another round of coffees.

Breytenbach, standing on the sidewalk, pushes the phone against his ear. The distorted voice at the end of the line seems especially menacing. "You've been avoiding me."

"I'm working," replies Breytenbach.

"Have you got the money?"

"I've got last month's payment. Still working on this month's."

"I need as much as you have."

"Just give me a couple more days, and I'll have more."

"I need it today. Put it in the usual place. I'll collect at six."

Breytenbach looks up at the sky. "Okay. Okay. Six."

"And you know what'll happen if it's not there."

"Yes."

"Or if you try to pull anything."

"Yes. It'll be there. But—"

"But what?"

"This is the last time."

"What do you mean, this is the last time? That's not your call. I'm the one who gets to decide when this is over."

"I will not do this anymore," says Breytenbach.

The person behind the AI-distorted voice is agitated. "You know what will happen if you stop the payments, right?"

"Yes."

"I'll post this video online, and everyone will know your dirty little secret."

"Please," begs Breytenbach. "Please, just leave me alone."

"I don't want you to beg. I want you to pay me, as per our arrangement."

"I can't have this hanging over me anymore. I can't do it."

"Pay up, and you'll have nothing to worry about."

20

SELL YOUR SOUL

"I OWE you so big time for this," says Jennifer Walker. She has a prime spot at the cordoned-off scene, courtesy of Swanepoel.

"Just don't tell anyone it came from me," he says.

"I'm so hot for you right now," she whispers into his ear. "Can I see you tonight? Same time, same place?"

It amuses Swanepoel. "They have a name for women like you, you know."

"Ambitious?" says Walker. "Opportunistic?"

"I was thinking more along the lines of ... lady of the night."

"Don't be an asshole, Swanepoel," Walker says. "I know it's difficult for you, but try."

"You know me so well. Too well. Sometimes it makes me worry about you."

"What do you mean?"

"Well, it makes me wonder ... what kind of woman would be with someone like me? What does it say about you? As a person?"

"Oh, spare me," says Jennifer, rolling her eyes. "Honestly. Spare me your self-reflecting self-loathing bullshit."

He grabs her elbow. "I'm being serious."

Walker jerks her arm away from his grip. "You know what, Swanepoel? You really know how to ruin things. You're like a pigeon on a goddamn chessboard. Call me when you're less full of your especially toxic brand of bullshit."

She strides towards her cameraman and adjusts her hair; applies a fresh coat of her signature red lipstick. "Ready?"

"Rolling," says the man.

"This morning, the dismembered body of Desiree Van Zyl was discovered here, at the back of this high-profile shopping centre. Miss Van Zyl was the second victim to be abducted and killed by the man who has been named *The Jigsaw Killer*. In the meantime, two other women, Emily Shuter and Denise Metlerkamp, went missing in the same manner as Longman and Van Zyl. The police are investigating every lead, but have no suspects so far. As always, we'll bring you every development as it happens. This is Jennifer Walker, reporting for ECN."

~

Parkview Police Station. 14th of July 2014, 11:58.

Swanepoel rushes in and sits at his desk.

"Nice of you to join us, Swanepoel," calls De Villiers.

"*Ja*, sorry."

"That's the third time this week," says the detective. "Don't make it a habit."

Breytenbach ambles up to De Villiers' desk. "Can I have a word?"

De Villiers lowers the file he's squinting at and looks at the lieutenant. "Shoot."

Breytenbach looks around. "Somewhere private?"

"O-o-o-o-h," says Swanepoel. "Breytenbach wants to get a room!"

They ignore Swanepoel's puerility.

"Sure," says De Villiers. "Let's go to the interrogation room."

They go in and close the door.

"What's up?" asks the detective.

"Devil ... I need ... I'd very much like a raise. Please."

De Villiers sighs. "*Ja*, Breytenbach, you and the rest of the world."

Breytenbach doesn't smile.

"You're in trouble?"

"No," says Breytenbach. "Yes. Kind of."

"Anything I can help with?"

Breytenbach scrubs his hair with his knuckles. "Apart from a raise? No."

"My budget for this year is already completely shot. We're actually over budget."

"Okay, I understand."

"Look," says De Villiers. "I'm not saying no. You're a hard worker. You're sharp. You're an asset to the force."

"Fat lot of good that does," says Breytenbach. "I work twelve-hour days, and I'm in debt up to my bloody eyeballs.

De Villiers sighs again. "Look. I'll make you a deal."

"Ha." He smiles, but De Villiers doesn't immediately get the joke.

"What?"

"I'm not sure that's a good idea. You know, making a deal with the devil."

"It's a good deal."

"I'm sure that's what the devil always says."

"This case we're working on. I'm under unbelievable pressure to stop this guy. We can't have someone ... okay, you know. You know the pressures—" he stops to rub his temples.

"Yes," says Breytenbach.

"So what I'm saying is: you're a good cop. Give me a reason to give you a raise. A proper raise, in the next budget."

The lieutenant looks slightly cheered. "So you're saying if I help solve this case—"

"Which, in theory, you should be doing, anyway—"

"But if I manage to crack it, you'll have something solid to motivate for at my next performance appraisal."

"Exactly. A promotion. A raise. And you don't even have to sell your soul."

On the way back to the office, they walk past Robin Susman, who is coming away from the coffee station with a steaming mug in her hand.

"Ah, detective Susman?" says Breytenbach.

"It's just 'Susman'."

"Sorry. Susman, I've got those records you asked for."

She frowns at him as he grabs them off his desk.

"The roll of all the people who had been in institutions in the relevant timeframe. Also, the list of all reported child abuse, whether it ended up in court or not. Most of it is on this flash drive here, but some entries haven't been captured yet. They only exist on paper." He holds up a stack of files.

"God, that's depressing," says Susman.

"What?"

"The size of that bloody list. It may as well be the Yellow Pages. We need to narrow it down. Put more coffee on, will you? And we'll get started."

"There must be a way to filter the data."

"Okay," says Susman. "Which other variables can we use?"

Breytenbach bites the end of the pen he's holding. "Common traits of serial killers: unstable home life, institutionalisation, which we have in the institution roll. Difficult relationship and or abuse from caregivers, which we have in the police reports. What else?"

"They show no empathy. Narcissistic. Problematic relationship with drugs and or booze."

"We'll probably only be able to find that in psych records. It's a long shot."

"Cruelty to animals. Pyromania."

"May be worth another police report search. The problem is that these things often go unnoticed and unreported. It's not a reliable variable."

"But it could work. It's worth a shot."

"Yes," agrees Susman. "But don't exclude the other data."

"I won't. I'll do this now and send you the long-list as soon as I have it."

Susman's phone vibrates in her pocket. She turns away from Breytenbach to answer it. "Susman here."

"Robin!" exclaims Clementine. "You sound exactly like your old self. All business. How are you holding up?"

"Well," replies Susman. "Relatively speaking."

"Problems with sleeping?"

Susman shakes her head. "No."

Clementine's surprised. "No?"

"Luckily, on this case, there's no time to sleep."

Clementine laughs. "That's grasping at straws if I've ever seen it."

"One grasps at what one can."

"Is there anything I can do? I want this bastard behind bars as much as any of you."

"No. But thanks for asking."

"You're sure?"

Susman takes a sip of her cold, bitter coffee, and grimaces. "Now that I think about it—"

"Anything, darling."

"You know we were joking about your Nespresso machine?"

"Don't say another word. I'll have a new one delivered to the station today."

"Thank you. I'm no coffee connoisseur, but I couldn't stand another day of this awful stuff they have here. Just let me know how much it costs."

"Don't be silly, Robin. I'll send the bill to Alastair!"

21

HANGMAN

MAJOR ALASTAIR DENTON picks up his telephone receiver and presses a button. "Denton here. It's a secure line."

"Major," says Smith. It's bedlam in the background. People are chanting and shouting.

"You have anything for me?"

"Excuse the noise on this side. I'm outside the courthouse. I have updates on the Whittaker case and Bombela."

"Those can wait. You have anything on the Turbine Hall Gang?"

"They're in court today. Right now. That's why I'm here."

"What's the feeling on the ground?" asks the major.

"It's difficult to say. The public hates them, you know that. There have been protesters here since sunrise, calling for the death penalty."

"Good," says Alastair.

"I thought you disliked the death penalty," says Smith.

"I find it abhorrent. But which judge will give parole to prisoners when the public are baying for their blood?"

"They'll be dead by dinnertime," says Smith.

"Exactly."

There's a knock on the door, and Denton rings off. Devil sticks his head in. "Sorry to interrupt you, Major."

Alastair's face darkens in anticipation. "Another abandoned baby? Or another body?"

"Another body, sir. But it's not one of the missing mothers. It's a new case."

"Who, then?"

"We haven't identified it yet. Forensics are busy with it, now. It seems to be another one of those cases that you hate, sir."

"What do you mean?"

"One that captures the public's imagination."

The major groans. "Oh, God. My phone's already ringing off the bloody hook. What do we know so far?"

"They found the body—a male body—hanging from an eToll gantry."

"Hanging from an eToll gantry?" asks the major. "Has the world gone mad?"

De Villiers sighs. "The world has always been mad."

"Hanging? So it may be suicide?"

"Doubt it, sir. Msibi said he was dead before they placed him there."

"He's not an official, is he? Don't tell me someone is so angry about eTolls they've done something like this."

"We can't say yet. At first, we all thought it was a grand gesture to the government. Or some dramatic protestation gone wrong. But now it looks like plain, old-fashioned murder."

The major clears his throat. "Do you ever feel that we are wasting our time?

"Catching killers?" De Villiers asks. "No."

"But even when we catch them," says Alastair, the muscles in his jaws working hard. "Look at the Turbine Hall Gang. They've got that ruthless lawyer, and now they may be days away from being back on the streets. After all we did, after all we went through to put them away."

"You're worried about Susman?" asks De Villiers. "She's doing okay."

"It looks like she is doing okay. There is a difference."

"You owe me a beer, Devil," says Msibi. "Susman paid up with the coffee. Now it's your turn."

"Beer?" says De Villiers into the phone. "Only one?"

"A six-pack. The expensive ones. Green bottles."

He looks at his watch. "It's a bit early in the day for that, isn't it?"

"*Haibo*, you've changed."

"So you've identified the hangman?"

"*Yebo*, Sir Detective. Affirmative."

"And?"

"And I've sent the file to that adorable intern of yours."

"Khaya's not an intern. He's a sergeant."

"He's adorable, anyway."

"He's happily married," says De Villiers.

"I didn't mean it that way."

"I know, you want to cuddle him. Like a puppy."

"Those big brown chocolate button eyes, how can you stand it?"

"Easily," says De Villiers.

"I want to *schmusch* his cheeks," says Msibi.

"I never figured you for the cuddling type."

"No? Have you not noticed my body? It's very voluptuous. It is made for cuddling."

De Villiers sighs. "Why are we even having this conversation? I don't have time to—"

"It's to keep things light, Captain. To help you with your headaches. To help me with my peptic ulcer. Life isn't all about the darkness, you now. Just because a joke's not important doesn't mean it's not worthwhile."

"Thanks for sending the file to Khaya. I'll call you if I have questions."

"Are you sure he's happily married?" asks Msibi.

"Khaya? Yes. Why?"

"Ah, nothing. Just reminded me of a joke."

"I'm listening," says De Villiers.

"I thought fancy detectives didn't have time for jokes?"

"It had better be funny."

"Well, it's not a joke-joke."

"Msibi," says De Villiers. "Get on with it."

"It's just something my uncle used to say. He was a funny guy. *I'd hate to be unhappily married,* he'd say, *because I'm happily married, and it's SHIT.*"

~

"Right, Khaya," says De Villiers. "Who's the hanging man?"

"I was just saying to detective Susman—"

"Not a detective," corrects Susman.

"I was asking if she would help us on this case, too."

"And she said no," says De Villiers.

Khaya nods.

"A middle-aged white man hanging off a gantry is not Susman's kind of case."

"Why not?"

"Because the victim is not a woman."

"You only care about women?" asks Khaya.

"It's not that," says Robin.

"You just care about women more than men?"

"No," she says. "It's complicated."

"She'll explain it to you one day, Khaya, when you're all grown up. In the meantime, tell me about our eToll man."

"His name is Richard Sterling."

De Villiers holds up his hand to stop Khaya from speaking and yells out to the rest of the office. "Swanepoel, Vellie, Breytenbach, Modise, come here. Listen here. This is your new case."

"I'll be there now," says Breytenbach. "I'm just in the middle of something important."

"Sounds promising," says the detective. "Better be."

Breytenbach nods.

De Villiers addresses the cops standing around his desk. "Before Khaya briefs you ... Swanepoel and Vellie, this case is yours. Code-name 'Hangman'. I need to focus on the Jigsaw Killer. You can report to me on developments."

They nod.

Khaya looks chuffed that he gets to brief the team. "The vic's name is Richard Sterling. He died of a head injury. No patterned abrasions and no brush-burn. Blunt force trauma. That means he was *klapped* over the head with something heavy."

"We know what 'blunt force trauma' means, Khaya," says Swanepoel.

"Why was he hanged?" asks De Villiers. "Was it to send a message?"

Swanepoel looks at the detective. "You think it's a warning? Drug lord? Mafia?"

De Villiers shrugs. "Could be. In any case, it's an interesting way to dispose of a body."

"From what I can tell, Sterling doesn't seem to be that kind of man," says Khaya.

De Villiers takes the file from him. "Please elaborate?"

"It's not like he was the owner of a strip club or anything. Nothing seedy, from the looks of it."

"Ask most members of the Mafia what they do for a living, and they say 'import/export'. They never say import of *what*. Never trust a man who says he's in 'import/export'."

"Okay," says Swanepoel. "So what did this Richard Sterling do, if his career has been so immaculate as not to make the very Devil suspicious?"

"He was a renowned surgeon," says Khaya.

"Ah. For once we come across someone who saves lives instead of taking them."

Khaya pulls a face. "Not quite."

"Not another Chris Barnard then? What kind of surgery? Bones? Teeth?"

"You're getting closer. He was a cosmetic surgeon."

"Cosmetic, like plastic surgery? Are we talking fixing kids' burn scars or sucking out rich housewives' cellulite?"

"The latter," says De Villiers. "And by the looks of it, he's done a lot of it in his time. He was a multi-millionaire. Owned a string of luxury bush 'escapes' where international tourists would come to visit and get their faces done. Instead of staying in New York with a bandaged-up face and having to avoid your friends and colleagues, you come to South Africa and have it done here by a top-notch surgeon. You pay in Rands and have two weeks of five-star downtime."

"Wow," says Swanepoel. "The lives of the rich and famous."

"Don't be envious, Swanepoel," says De Villiers. "Being rich isn't always what it's cracked up to be."

"And you would know this, how?"

De Villiers smirks. "Clearly not from personal experience."

"Devil is right. Imagine all the stress. The bond repayments on all the different houses all over the world. The helicopter maintenance—"

"*Ja*, well," says Swanepoel. "I got ninety-nine problems and being rich ain't one of them."

"At the end of the day, us sorry sacks sitting here are better off than Mr Sterling," De Villiers says, shrugging. "At least we're alive."

"Good point," says Swanepoel.

"So," Devil rubs his hands together. "A mega-wealthy man is murdered. Who do we look at first?"

"The wife," says Khaya.

"Yes."

"And then the business partners."

"Yes. And the competitors, and the enemies."

"She's here," Khaya gestures at the passage. "The wife. Mrs Sterling is in Room Three."

"That was quick," says De Villiers.

"She came in herself. Wanted to talk."

"Well, men. It looks like this case may solve itself if we're lucky. Swanepoel, you're the good-looking one. You do the talking. You know the drill, start by taking it easy, be empathetic. Befriend her. Coax her into a solid confession. Try not to alienate her with your bullshit."

"Ah, Devil, I never knew you felt that way about me."

"Don't get excited, Swanepoel. You're not my type. Take Khaya with you. He needs to learn. Don't teach him anything shifty, okay? He's still an Innocent."

Breytenbach slams his phone down in excitement.

De Villiers looks up. "You have something?"

"More than 'something,'" Breytenbach says. "I think I have ... I mean it's premature to say. I'll take you through my thinking and how—"

"I'm getting old here, Breytenbach," says De Villiers. "What? What do you think you know?"

Breytenbach takes a deep breath; his eyes sparkle with excitement. He stares at De Villiers. "I think I might have him. The Jigsaw Killer."

22

A NAME OF A GHOST

PARKVIEW POLICE STATION, **16th of July 2014, 9:12.**

"Tell me," says detective De Villiers.

Breytenbach hammers at his keyboard; it's an old thing that crunches as he types. "I'm printing his file. The system is trying to find his address. No luck so far. Putting his picture up on the screen now."

They wait a few breaths, then a photo of a young man appears on the monitor: dark hair, dark eyebrows, sharp cheekbones and chin. A small crucifix hangs from a gold chain around his neck.

"He's better looking than I expected," says De Villiers.

Susman folds her arms. "They usually are."

"What is that on his cheek?" asks De Villiers. "A scar?"

"Looks like a small burn mark. A cigarette?"

"Breytenbach. You found the other variable."

The lieutenant looks excited.

"Variable?" asks Khaya.

"This institution roll was too long to work through. Not at the speed we needed to find this guy. So I tried other variables to triangulate the data. I struck out any names that didn't have a criminal record. That halved the pile. Then I checked those records for cruelty to animals and pyromania and got a shortlist. No one on that list was our guy."

"How do you know?" asks Khaya.

"Some are dead, others still institutionalised or in prison. A few live out of the country. Our guy wasn't there."

"Okay," says De Villiers.

"So then I went back to the criminal record list and looked for victims of possible child abuse. Not surprisingly, this didn't make much of a dent."

"So you added another criterion," says Susman.

"I had a brainwave. Last year, my washing machine packed up."

"Make your point, Breytenbach." De Villiers fidgets. "I can't sit in this chair for much longer knowing that we might have this guy."

"The system is still searching. I don't think he has an address on file."

Susman's paying attention. "Your washing machine packed up?"

"Yes. So I went to a hyper store to buy a new one. And I couldn't put it in my car, right? So they had to deliver."

"So you had to give them your address," says Susman.

"Address, phone number, ID number."

"ID number?" asks De Villiers.

"For insurance. The guarantee."

"So this guy bought an appliance recently?"

Susman's face opens up. "Of course he did. A chest freezer."

De Villiers' lips curl into a smile.

"So I called all the hyper stores in Gauteng. Asked for customers who bought a chest freezer in the last couple of years. I cross-referenced that with my shortlist and got just one hit."

"That's him," says Khaya. "It's gotta be him, right?"

"The details given were actually of an older woman, a Brenda Flock. It was just the surname that matched. She is deceased, has been for a decade."

"So unless a dead woman was out shopping for kitchen appliances..."

"He used his mother's details on the store's forms. Probably just made up a story about how he was buying a gift for his mom."

"First name?" asks Susman.

"David. David Flock."

De Villiers stares at the screen. "Why is this taking so long?"

"Usually when it takes this long, it means there's no address on file," says Breytenbach.

"Of course," says De Villiers. "That would have been too easy."

"It's funny, isn't it?" asks Susman, looking intensely at the crucifix. "The surname?"

De Villiers shoots her a glance. "Maybe to a sheep farmer."

"Flock of sheep, like believers?" says Khaya. "Like Jesus takes care of his flock?"

"Exactly," says Susman. "Here is this man named David—a biblical name—who seeks to control people, as a religious leader does. He expects his mother to be pure, virginal. Anything else makes her a Fallen Woman. Maybe he is building his own version of the perfect mother, piece by piece. Creating her from others' bodies, like the story of Adam's rib, in Genesis. He sees himself as a kind of god, giving life and taking it away."

"A religious bent makes sense," says Breytenbach. "As a child, he was removed by social services and put in the care of a Christian group—The Parable People—when Brenda Flock was arrested for soliciting."

"Soliciting?" asks Devil. "Flock's mother was a prostitute?"

"A single mother, no maintenance from the child's father," says Susman. "She did what she had to, to keep food on the table."

"She also left him in others' care for extended periods while she went partying. She'd disappear for days at a time. Not much family to speak of."

"He would have seen that as abandonment," says Susman.

"It was abandonment," replies De Villiers. "What about the abuse?"

"The Parable People," says Breytenbach.

Susman shivers. "It sounds like some kind of cult."

"They reported injuries. Bruises, broken bones. Cigarette burns. There's no photographic evidence, though. The mother denied it, said it was the Parable People who had abused him. Brainwashed him."

"That scar," says Khaya. "That scar under his eye."

"It could be from anything," says Susman. "Where does the carpentry thing come in?"

"Well, Jesus was a carpenter," says De Villiers.

Susman smiles.

"I don't know," says Breytenbach. "No carpentry jobs in his record. No jobs at all. He seems to be a drifter." The computer beeps. No address found.

"But he would have to have a woodwork room," says Susman. "Some tools. The jigsaw, for one."

"And maybe it's soundproofed to a certain extent if it's in a residential area. So he'd be able to do the noisy work without raising complaints. Or suspicion."

"Which means he'd be able to keep a prisoner there."

Susman feels an awful tingle moving along her spine. They're getting closer; they have a name of a ghost.

"Not only is there no address, but no employment history, no credit cards, no bank account. How does he live, day to day? It's like he doesn't even exist."

"Is he using his mother's details, his mother's bank account?"

"No," says Breytenbach. "It was frozen years ago."

Devil can't help smiling, even though he knows it's in bad taste. "Excuse the pun."

Swanepoel arrives. "Hey, what's going on in here? You guys all look like naughty little school kids trying not to laugh. Is it the new coffee that's made you so happy?"

"Big break in the Jigsaw case," says De Villiers. "No thanks to you."

"I was busy with the newly widowed Mrs Sterling. Did you forget that you asked me to interview her?"

"What did she say?"

"*Jussis*," says Swanepoel. "What didn't she say?"

"What does that mean? Did you get a confession?"

"Not a confession so much as a scolding. She's pissed off that we haven't found who did it yet, and says she knows people in high places that can get us all fired if we don't do our jobs properly. Says she was at the spa when it happened, in the floatation tank."

"Do you believe her?"

"Her face is so paralysed by Botox, it was tough to tell. It's like talking to a shop mannequin. Seriously. Like, her eyebrows don't move. But that's not all. That's not the interesting part. She's got a record."

"A criminal record?" asks De Villiers.

"No, although maybe she should have. She has a record of dead husbands."

Breytenbach whistles.

"Sterling was her fifth husband. All the others kicked the bucket while married to her."

Susman pipes up. "So either she's the world's unluckiest bride or ... she's a brilliant husband-killer."

"Hey!" scolds De Villiers. "You're not supposed to be listening. This isn't your case."

"It's so difficult to tell if she is lying," says Swanepoel. "She's had so much plastic surgery I'm surprised that her face doesn't melt in the sun. She's like a ... a robot. An angry robot."

"What does the lover say?" asks Susman.

Khaya frowns. "How do you know she has a lover?"

"This kind of woman always has a lover," says De Villiers.

"Well, there's this guy: Ian Paviel. He's a partner at Sterling Safaris. He seems to have taken a chopper and disappeared."

"Hmm." De Villiers shifts in his chair. "You keeping her in custody?"

"Nah. Had to let her go. Have nothing on her."

"Yet," says De Villiers. "Give them a couple of hours. I'm quite sure they'll be running into the sunset together."

Swanepoel snorts. "I'd watch my back if I were him!"

The detective's phone rings. *"Yebo,"* he says, then turns away from the others to hide his grimace. *"Ja,* was expecting that. We'll be there now."

He ends the call and rubs his forehead.

"Not another one," says Susman. "Not so soon!"

De Villiers turns back to the group. "Dismembered body of Emily Shuter found half an hour ago, in a *spruit* in Craighall Park. Missing her arms, hands."

"Damn it. The window is shrinking fast. That means he's going to take someone else very soon if he hasn't already."

"Before, it was one woman a week," says Khaya. "Now? Why is he speeding up so much?"

"It's very common to see serial killers escalate like this," says De Villiers. "They get addicted to the climax of killing. It's like a drug: the comedown after the high is bad, so he needs to start his process again as soon as possible to get that high again. The more he does it, the easier the process is. Less planning, less hesitation."

"At the same time, he realises the more women he kills, the more likely he is to be caught. He has to finish his project before anyone can stop him. It's become everything to him. It's all-consuming."

"So ... he might stop? On his own, I mean? When he's finished his project?"

"No," says Susman. "His urge to kill will be the same. He'll probably fine-tune his sculpture. Start looking at the details: fingers. Eyes. It's something he could carry on tweaking *ad infinitim.*"

"Every moment counts, now," says De Villiers. "Let's get going. Susman, you up for this?"

"My counsellor told me no more dead bodies."

"Since when do you listen to anyone?" asks the detective, weighing the car keys in his hand.

Susman stands up. "That's what I said."

23

LAMBS INSTEAD OF BABIES

THE NEWS ANCHOR on the radio station in De Villiers' car is relentless. "Israeli tanks, infantry and engineering units were ordered to launch a broad front assault on Gaza by the prime minister Binyamin Netanyahu as last-ditch efforts to secure a ceasefire deal in Cairo collapse. Launching the assault..."

De Villiers turns the volume down.

"I have *déjà vu*, says Susman. "Weren't we doing this exact same thing a couple of days ago? Wasn't the news report identical?"

"Every day is the same. This many rockets, this many fatalities. Peace talks. Ceasefires. More rockets, more deaths. It never stops."

"Gaza Groundhog Day," says Robin. "I don't know how you bear to listen."

"How can I not?"

His phone rings and Khaya offers to answer it for him. "It's the station."

De Villiers nods.

"Hi, Khaya here. Devil's driving." He listens. "That's bad. That's very bad, hey. Okay. I'll tell him."

De Villiers speeds up. "What?"

Khaya's voice is quiet. "Another baby found. Without his mother."

"Where?"

"Linden."

"Turn around," says Susman.

"We can't," says Devil. "We have to see the new body at the *spruit*."

"Let Msibi take care of the body. She can handle it. We'll swing by later. I want to go to the scene of the crime. I need to get closer to him. Feel him." The hair on the back of her neck stands up.

"Khaya, get the Linden address." De Villiers slows down and does a U-turn. A taxi driver leans on his hooter as he drives past. "Tell them we'll be there in fifteen minutes."

~

Bosman residence, Linden, 16th of July 2014, 10:21.

The three of them stand on the lawn of Carey Bosman's property in Linden. The atmosphere is frantic. Above the sirens, you can hear a baby wailing. They snap on their police-issue latex gloves as they talk.

"Who called it in?" asks De Villiers.

"I don't know." Khaya shakes his head. "A consultant? I didn't catch everything over the phone."

"A consultant?" asks Susman. "A colleague?"

"I don't know."

"Was it perhaps a lactation consultant?"

"Yes. Yes, that sounds right."

"Okay," says Susman, steeling herself. "Social worker here?"

"She's here already. There," he points. "She's the one holding the baby."

The baby is inconsolable. Susman walks over to the social worker and opens her arms. "May I?"

The woman looks surprised. "Badge?"

De Villiers flashes his. "She's with me."

Robin takes the distressed baby and rocks him gently, applying just enough pressure to make him feel safe. She coos to him as tears prick her eyes. "Hello, you poor thing. Poor mite. You miss your mom. I know. Shush. You'll be okay." The baby is still screaming, but he looks at Susman and grabs her hand. "Where's your dummy? Where's your blankie? Here it is. Here we go. There's a good baba." She pops the pacifier into his mouth and covers him with a soft blanket, positioning a corner near his face so he can feel the familiar fabric on his cheek. She keeps rocking and cooing until the baby's eyes roll back and he sleeps.

"You're a natural," says De Villiers. She hears the regret in his voice, knowing that she will never have a baby of her own.

"I have lambs now, instead of babies." She deflects the rush of emotion; now is not the time for pity.

De Villiers tries to lighten the mood. "Sheep are probably a better investment. Financially speaking."

Baby still in her arms, Susman turns to Khaya. "Do we know what time she was taken?"

"We're estimating between eight and half-past nine. The consultant said that she got here at ten and the baby was howling as if it had been alone for hours."

"*He*," says Susman.

"Yes. As if *he* had been alone for hours. But Bosman's mother called her this morning at around eight, and all was fine."

Susman passes the sleeping baby back to the social worker. "Khaya, bag that dummy."

"Really?"

"Yes, really. Bag all the pacifiers you see."

"Shame, can't he just keep that one he has in his mouth?"

"No. Bag it."

They gear up and head inside while press photographers snap pictures from the road. The house feels crowded. "De Villiers," says Susman. "There are too many people here. I can't think."

"Vellie, keep those damn vultures back, will you? Don't let them encroach on the scene. It would be a disaster for forensics. Right back! More than that. Okay. Put up more tape and handcuff anyone who breaches it. Matabane, Peters, Tshab, out of the house. Don't look at me like that! Go get a coffee or something."

Once the men leave, and the press is beaten back, there's more space to think.

"Better. Much better. Thank you."

"Okay. So this is Carey Bosman's house. Thirty-three-year-old white female, mother to five-week-old Timothy."

"Single mother. Brunette. Average height?"

"Affirmative," De Villiers nods.

"Packed a suitcase."

"It looks like it, yes. Her toiletries are gone."

"Why is he still bothering with the suitcase thing?" asks Khaya. "He knows we know he's taking the women. They are not abandoning their babies. Why carry on? It just takes more time."

"He has moved past the rational," says Susman. "His psychic break may be continuous. It's a ritual now. It won't feel right if he changes the routine." She's walking through the house, absorbing every detail she can. "A serial killer follows a psychological cycle for each kill. First is what they call the 'aura': the break from reality that allows him into his psychotic world where it is acceptable to murder. The second is trolling: searching for the right victim. After that, the stalking, the climax—murder—and then the low, or depression, which makes him want to start the cycle again. The way Flock is acting, it looks like he hasn't surfaced from his break in reality, it's become this intense trip for him. He's on a roll, and he'll keep going."

"Maybe that's a good thing," ventures Khaya. "Maybe he'll make a mistake now."

"He's already made mistakes," says Susman. "We just need to find them."

"How is he identifying these women?" asks Devil. "How is he selecting them?"

"I checked the online dating thing. None of the women were doing it."

"How else could he be doing it?"

Susman looks at a gadget on the kitchen counter. "What about this?"

"What is that?" asks Khaya.

"It's a breast pump. Khaya, check which brands and types the other mothers had. Could it be someone who works at the distribution office? Usually, you don't just pick these up off the shelf. You go in, and they help you choose the right model and teach you how to use it."

Khaya scribbles in his notebook. "I'll check."

"Also check out the lactation consultant."

De Villiers is inspecting the contents of the fridge, then closes it. On the door, ultra-sound pictures of the baby are held there by rubber fruit magnets, along with a hand-written sleeping and feeding schedule, and a pamphlet for The Good Food Truck.

"What about this pamphlet?" he says. Susman and Khaya glance over. De Villiers reads the copy out loud. "The Good Food Truck delivers healthy pre-cooked meals to people who are too busy to cook for themselves, too ill, or—"

"Let me guess," says Susman. "New mothers?"

"Yes."

"I'll check that right now," says Khaya, dialling the station's number.

De Villiers continues to read. "Delivers to Parkhurst, Greenside, Craighall, Linden, Parkview, Parktown North, Rosebank."

"That's our guy's area," says Susman.

"Breytenbach," says Khaya, into the phone. "I need you to check something for me urgently, please. Two things."

Susman's eyes are alight. "Why didn't we think of this before?"

"The Good Food Truck?" says De Villiers. "I've never heard of it before today. There were no menus in the other women's houses. No record on their credit cards pointing to this."

"No, I don't mean just the Food Truck. I mean *deliveries*. It's so obvious."

"Deliveries?"

"To single mothers with babies."

"When we had Niel, there was no such thing as The Good Food Truck. We used to eat frozen meals and take-aways because there was no time to cook dinner."

"Exactly. And there were two of you to care for him. Now imagine someone doing it on their own."

Khaya turns back to them. "Negative on the breast pumps," he says. "They didn't all use pumps. Those who did used different brands. And negative on The Good Food Truck. They only opened for business a couple of days ago. None of the victims' addresses are on their database. Maybe the flyer came in through the letterbox."

"Damn it," swore De Villiers. "I thought we had him."

"We might still have him," says Susman.

Khaya and De Villiers stare at her. "What do you mean?"

"So we agree that when you're a single mother of an infant, there's no time to cook, right?"

"Yes."

"There's no time to do anything. What else would you have delivered, if you could?"

"Nappies," says Khaya. "I remember going out for diapers in the middle of the night more than once."

"Yes. Nappies. What else?"

"Groceries."

"But specifically for new mothers?" prompts Susman.

"Nappies, wipes, creams, drops. You know, those drops?"

"Colic drops," says De Villiers.

"And where do you get all those things?"

"The pharmacy," says Khaya. "Or the baby shop."

"These days, you order online, and everything is delivered, right?"

"Look for waybill receipts," says De Villiers. "Look for boxes. Brown corrugated boxes."

"They've already searched the house," says Khaya. "They would have already seen a big empty box."

"There's a compost bucket, on the kitchen counter," says De Villiers.

"So?"

"So, I'll bet you a thousand bucks she recycles."

Khaya understands what the detective is implying, and runs out to check the wheelie bins in the courtyard.

Susman can feel they're on the right track. It energises her. "This is it. This is him. A delivery man. A courier. It's perfect, isn't it? He gets addresses of mothers literally handed to him. He can take his time to observe and select."

"And easiest of all: he gets to ring the doorbell and just walk right in," says De Villiers. "That's why there's no forced entry."

"All these security measures," says Susman. "The burglar bars, the high walls, the alarms. But if you order online, your delivery arrives, and you open your door to a complete stranger."

"Clever," says De Villiers.

Khaya rushes back in, holding a collapsed empty box like a trophy. "I've got it. I've got it. There are plenty of these boxes, from the same company. It's called BabyCo."

Susman looks at De Villiers. "Not clever enough."

24

LONE WOLVES

"You've got him?" asks Major Denton.

"We're close," says Devil. "We've got his M.O. and BabyCo. gave us their list of employees. Drivers. And all their customers. We have their full co-operation. No subpoena necessary. They've cancelled all deliveries until further notice and have emailed customers to not let anyone into their houses."

"That's not good enough," says the major. "They need to phone every one of those customers to warn them. If there are any they can't get hold of, we'll send escorts."

Khaya nods. "Yes, sir, Major."

"Why didn't we pick this up sooner? We had their credit card statements, didn't we?"

"BabyCo. accepts cash on delivery, electronic transfer and card payments, so it didn't show up as a common denominator on their bank statements."

The major excuses himself to make some calls.

"There's no 'David Flock' on BabyCo.'s payroll," says Khaya.

"So he's using a fake name?" asks De Villiers.

"Either that or Flock isn't our guy."

"He can't be using a fake name," says Khaya. "BabyCo. requires full FICA before they hire. ID book, proof of residency, proof of bank account. It all has to match up. A bank won't give you an account on a made-up name."

"How many drivers service our area?"

"Between three and five, depending on how busy it gets. Two of the drivers were working on all five days the victims were taken. It's one of them."

"Not necessarily," says Susman.

"I don't follow."

"If you were the killer, would you take someone when you were on duty, possibly compromising your day's work, causing suspicion? Or would you do it on your day off?"

Khaya nods, conceding Robin's point.

"All he needed was his uniform and badge, a nondescript van, and a BabyCo. box. A fake waybill, a clipboard."

The sergeant is tapping on his laptop. "Let's see. Okay, there was only one driver who wasn't working on all of those days the women were abducted. Cadenhead. Zachary."

Breytenbach walks in. "Heard you guys had a breakthrough."

"Zack Cadenhead," says De Villiers. "Why does that sound familiar?"

Khaya jumps in his seat. "Cadenhead's address is 283 Rosebank Heights."

"Cadenhead?" asks Breytenbach. "I also remember the name. I'll check my files."

"Khaya, send the nearest unit to Cadenhead's address now. We'll follow if they find anything."

"What about Flock?" asks Khaya.

Devil looks at the sergeant. "Flock's a ghost."

"Breytenbach," says Susman. "Pull up Cadenhead's file, will you? I'm interested to know why he didn't make your shortlist."

The lieutenant jumps onto Khaya's laptop and smashes the keyboard. "Oh, shit, look. Here he is. He was on my long list, but didn't make the final pick."

"Remind me?"

"The long list was previously institutionalised, plus a criminal record. Cadenhead didn't make the shortlist because there is no history of childhood abuse."

"So he was institutionalised," says Susman. "For what?"

"Drug abuse. That's why he had a record, too. Was arrested for possession when he was fifteen, seventeen and twenty-one. Minor offences— just a user, nothing more—and his record was expunged. That's probably why BabyCo. didn't pick it up when they hired him. He had a clean record by then."

"Where was he put?" asks Susman. "Which institution?"

"Bergview Boys. It's a juvenile detention centre in Magaliesberg. Hang on—"

De Villiers spins his chair to face Breytenbach. "What?"

"Bergview Boys. Holy shit."

Susman and Devil stare at him.

"That's where ... I think that's where Flock went, too. Let me check."

"Wait, they know each other? Flock and Cadenhead?"

"Holy ... yes. Their stays overlapped by a year in 1992. And ... shit, you'll never believe this."

Susman narrows her eyes. "Land the plane, Breytenbach."

"They were in the same woodwork class."

"They're ... what? In this together? Working as a team?" asks De Villiers.

Susman shakes her head. "It would be very unusual. I'd say, almost impossible. Serial killers are, inherently, lone wolves."

"But maybe when two lone wolves meet, and they enjoy doing the same thing ... then they stick together."

"They help each other. They're a team. Things are easier when there are two of you."

"It's creepy," says Breytenbach. "They even look similar. They could be twins, or at the very least, brothers."

"Is it possible that they are both psychopaths, and that's what allowed them to connect?"

"I'm not saying it's impossible," says Susman. "Just highly unlikely. Serial killers are anti-social, narcissistic, selfish. They don't play nicely with others. They certainly don't like sharing."

"But it has been known to happen," says De Villiers. "Bonny and Clyde. Aileen Wuornos and partner."

"There's no point in speculating," says Susman. "The important thing is to move on this as quickly as we can."

"Vellie and Swanepoel were just down the road from Cadenhead's apartment. They should be there already. I'm sure they'll call in any second."

"What about Cadenhead's mother?" asks Susman.

"Alive and well. Professional. Living in Parktown North. Couldn't be more different from Flock's mother."

"Call her. Get whatever you can from her. Their relationship. Her opinion of his current state of mind."

Breytenbach looks up the number and dials.

"Hello?" says a sophisticated voice.

"Good afternoon, Mrs Cadenhead. It's Lieutenant Breytenbach speaking, from the Parkview—"

"Lieutenant?"

"Lieutenant Breytenbach, from the Parkview Police—"

"Oh my God," the woman whispers. "Oh, my God. It's finally happened, hasn't it?"

Breytenbach hesitates. "I beg yours?"

"He's ... dead, isn't he? He's finally killed himself."

"Mrs Cadenhead—"

"Where is he? I want to see him. Oh," she cries. "Oh, Jeremy. Jeremy! Come here! They've found Zack!"

"Mrs Cadenhead, please. Calm down."

The woman is crying loudly now. She drops the receiver and Breytenbach can hear her retching. "You take the phone!" she exclaims. "It's the police."

A male voice comes on the line. "Hello?"

"Mr Cadenhead? Jeremy Cadenhead?"

"Speaking. You've found our boy?"

"We're looking for him. We thought you might help."

"You're *looking* for him? What do you mean? Does that mean you stopped looking for him, before now?"

"Hold on," says Breytenbach. "I think we need to start again."

"I don't understand what's going on," says Mrs Cadenhead in the background.

"What is there to say?" says an emotional Mr Cadenhead. "My son has been missing for the last two years and you bloody police never seem to have a bloody clue what is going on. That's why we hired Price. Because we knew you lot would never find him. Never find him alive, anyway. Because that's why you're calling now, isn't it? Because you've found his body?"

"You're saying that your son Zachary has been missing for two years?"

"Are you saying you've found him?"

"Who is 'Price'?" asks Breytenbach.

"He's the P.I. we hired."

"Can you please give me his contact details?"

"Not before you tell me what the bloody hell is going on! Have you found our boy or not?"

"Mr Cadenhead. Please, sit down. I will tell you what I know."

25

CRUELLA

KHAYA HOLDS his phone to his chest. "Devil? Swanepoel just called. They're at Cadenhead's residence. Zack's not there. They need a comprehensive forensic team sent over immediately."

"Bodies?" asks De Villiers.

"Sound-proofed, refrigerated workshop, jigsaw, tools, chest freezer. And, yes, bodies. Metlerkamp, he thinks. And Bosman. He said it's like a scene from a horror movie. He wants you to call him."

De Villiers throws down the papers he has in his hands. "Okay people, listen up!"

The office quietens down.

"I know it seems like we have this guy, but he's still out there. He may be stalking his next victim as we speak. There is a young mother and her baby who we need to keep together. I want you to all to keep calm, put your heads down, and do what it takes to finish this guy."

"Khaya," says Susman. "Find out if Cadenhead was using the BabyCo. delivery van or his own vehicle. Registration plates for both must be sent to every cop in Jo'burg."

"Yes, Ma'am."

Msibi waltzes in. "My trio! My tribe."

"Msibi," says De Villiers. "What the hell are you doing here?"

"That's not what you said in bed last night, l-l-lover."

De Villiers gives her a look of disapproval.

Khaya chuckles. "She's just messing with you, Devil."

Msibi winks at Khaya, who blushes. "Hello, puppy-love."

De Villiers isn't in the mood for joking. "Seriously, what are you doing here? Shouldn't you be heading over to the scene? We're under the gun here."

"*Ag* Devil, you're so cute when you're stressed. Watch out, or that vein in your head will pop right out of your forehead and strangle you!"

Susman looks at Msibi. "I'm assuming you have something for us?"

"Of course! Why else would I be here? Your guys' company isn't that scintillating. I'm on my way to Rosebank, by the way, Devil. So you can stop twitching."

"What do you have?"

"Well, I heard that a certain woman—a very *cruel* woman—took the dummy out of a poor little baby's mouth this morning. After all he'd been through! What kind of woman does that, Khaya? I ask you. Poor little sad baby finally stops crying and 'PLOP'! she takes his dummy!"

"A ... genius woman?" asks De Villiers.

"That's right, Devil! That's right! A genius woman!"

Susman's heart beats faster. "You found something on the dummy?"

"*Yebo*, Cruella. A partial print."

"How partial?"

"Enough for a five-point match to one ... David Flock."

"So they must be working together," says Khaya.

"I'll leave the pontificating up to you. I'm off to Cadenhead's flat. From what I've heard, it'll be my new nightmare fuel. Thank God. I was getting bored with the old ones! Are you lot coming, or not?"

~

Cadenhead residence, Rosebank Heights, 16th of July 2014, 14:29.

Zack Cadenhead's residence is cold and eerie; the soundproofing adds to the claustrophobia. The loudest sound is the camera's shutter. The constant flashing of light on the gory masterpiece in the centre of the room makes Susman feel unsteady. The flesh sculpture is, in its own way, magnificent—if you can call something so macabre magnificent. Every limb is purposefully angled, every stitch and bolt is perfectly placed. It's a brutal take on Michelangelo's Pietà: Madonna and son, but it's terribly incomplete. The mother has neither a head nor a child.

Khaya rubs his arms to keep warm. He speaks quietly to Susman. "Exactly as you said."

"What?" she asks.

"A sound-proof room. Carpentry tools. And right in the centre, his—"

Susman swallows hard. "His creation. His re-creation of his mother."

"The most horrible thing I've ever seen. You?"

Susman doesn't reply.

Khaya looks at her, wide-eyed. "Please don't tell me you've seen something worse than this."

She looks away. "I wish I could."

They're quiet while they inspect the room.

"Times like this," says Khaya.

"Yes?"

"It just makes me wonder about people. About how sick humankind is."

Susman sighs. "Don't extrapolate the evil of one man, or a couple of men, Khaya. It's not true, and it doesn't serve anyone. Most humans don't torture; don't kill."

"I guess we get a skewed perception, doing what we do."

"Doing what *you* do," she says. "I can't wait to get back to my sheep."

"On days like today ... looking at this *thing,* I feel like asking you if I can come with you. I grew up in the country, you know. I know how to handle livestock. I know about sheep."

"Well, in that case, you have an open invitation to visit."

"Really?"

"Really. I always need more hands. Your kids would love it, and I promise I won't wave my shotgun around."

"Hey," says Khaya, inspecting a mark on the side-table. "Look here."

"What's that?"

"It's, like, his signature. It's on all the furniture."

"What does it say?"

"*Vlokkie?* A version of his surname? Like Afrikaans? Little Flock?"

"Or little flake," says Susman. "*Vlokkie.*"

"Nickname?"

"I'm guessing his mother used to call him that. Like, her little snowflake."

"That's sweet," says Khaya. "Like her calling him beautiful and unique. It doesn't sound like something an abusive mother would do."

"It may have been part of the abuse."

"Hey?"

"Part of her manipulation of him."

"And now ... now he is manipulating her, in his own way."

They look again at the sculpture in the middle of the room, grimacing.

"Literally."

"It looks like Frankenstein," says Khaya.

"Frankenstein's monster," says Susman. "Frankenstein was the doctor. The creator. Not the monster. He took pride in it, you can see. Look at the details. Look how he tried to match the parts exactly, how he shaved the edges to line up. How he grafted skin over the joins and the staples."

Perhaps she's too close to the gory creation; she feels unsteady and steps back.

"Are you okay?"

She takes a deep breath, but it doesn't help. "Dizzy," she says.

"Susman?" asks De Villiers. She can see him coming over to her, but her vision is bright, stretched and surreal.

"Fine," she says. "I'm fine."

Breytenbach has Flock's laptop. "This is how he stalked his victims. He'd get their names and addresses from the BabyCo. waybills, then check them out on Facebook. He could find everything he needed to know there. Marital status, hair and eye colour, age of the infant. This is where he would identify the women that looked like his mother."

"You're talking about Flock. Flock's mother. What about Cadenhead? Where does he fit in?"

"From what I can tell, Cadenhead's parents are loving and supportive," says Breytenbach. "The parental relationship doesn't match the profile of a violent psychopath at all. No history of abandonment or abuse. No previous violence of any kind on Zack's record. The parents are caring. Respectful. When the P.I. they hired stopped taking their calls, they stopped looking. They concluded that Zack didn't want to be found."

"What are you saying? You don't think Cadenhead did it? Despite all this?" De Villiers gestures to the human flesh sculpture in the middle of the room.

"I don't know. Is it possible that Flock was paying him to help? Cadenhead has a long history of drug abuse. Addicts always need money; maybe he was desperate? Desperate enough to do what Flock asked?"

Susman can't feel her fingers anymore. She tries to take another step backwards, but her knees are jelly.

"Susman," says De Villiers. "You're pale. Why don't you sit down?"

When it looks like she might faint, he grabs hold of her elbow and steers her out of the room.

26

A PILE OF ROCKS

"KHAYA," prompts De Villiers. "Get Susman a glass of water."

"No," Susman says, pale as ice.

"It'll make you feel better."

Khaya is stuck mid-exit, not sure who to listen to.

"No," Susman shakes her head. "I don't want to drink out of anything this man has touched."

"Should we leave?" the detective asks. "We've seen enough. The team will report back."

"No. I need to be here." She feels the torrential wave of panic about to knock into her. "Just leave me alone for a few minutes, will you? I can feel it coming. I just need to get through it."

De Villiers' phone vibrates in his pocket. It's Anna-Mart. He answers it, turning away from Susman and nodding at Khaya to go.

"André!" cries his wife.

"Anna-Mart? What's happened?"

"I got a call."

De Villiers feels an instant tension headache wrap around his temple; cold steel. "From Niel? A call from Niel?"

"About Niel," sobs Anna-Mart.

He gulps down some air, reminds himself to stay calm.

"It was from Clive."

"Clive?"

"The man who organises the Kibbutz stays. He helped us place Niel."

"What did he say?"

Anna-Mart cries harder. He feels he will drown in her sobs.

"Damn it, Anna, what did he say?"

"He's been trying to get hold of the Kibbutz for days. No answer. Then today he got a call from one of his colleagues over there. It's been hit, André, it's been hit!"

Fear slows his brain. "What's been hit?"

"The kibbutz!"

"Hit?" Maybe he needs her to spell it out for him because the reality isn't sinking in.

"Bombed! It's been bombed. He said ... his words were ... 'there's nothing left'."

"How many people were—" He clears his throat and starts again. "Were there any casualties?"

"They haven't found any ... bodies yet."

"That's good news?"

"Yet, André, yet. It's a pile of rocks."

"I'll book the next flight out."

"You can't. They've cancelled all flights to Israel."

De Villiers scrabbles desperately to feel useful. He can't stand feeling out of control when the stakes are so high. "There must be something I can do."

A tap on his shoulder spins him around. Breytenbach. "We've found something."

De Villiers holds his palm up, gesturing for the lieutenant to wait for him. He whispers into the phone. "What can I do, Anna-Mart?"

"Nothing," she says. She has stopped crying now. "Nothing. We have to wait."

"This is impossible," he says, pulling on his hair.

"I don't want to see anybody but you."

"I'll come over as soon as I can. Will probably only be late tonight."

"I'll wait up," she says.

"*Yussis*," says Breytenbach, once Devil ends the call. "Are you okay, Devil? Susman? You two look like you've just seen a ghost."

De Villiers looks over to Robin. She's spooked, but breathing normally. He wonders how many panic attacks she deals with, how much it must erode her. Suddenly wishes he had never taken her from her sheep farm. He swallows the obstruction in his throat. Susman and De Villiers follow Breytenbach through to another room, where Msibi is waiting for them with a grim expression on her face. Humming softly against the wall is a large chest freezer.

"Ah, Breytenbach," murmurs Susman. "Here is your lucky chest freezer."

Msibi opens the lid with her gloved hands, and cold vapour spills out of the white box as if she is performing a magic trick on a stage. They approach cautiously to look inside as if something might jump out at them.

"Lucky for me," says Breytenbach. "Not so lucky for—"

Msibi lifts a transparent freezer bag containing a severed head, and Susman flinches. "Cadenhead?" she guesses.

"*Yebo*," says the lieutenant. "And he's not the only male body in here. I'm assuming the other body is Price, the private investigator Zack's parents hired to find him."

Msibi nods. "Judging by the freezer burn I'd guess Price has been here a year, and Cadenhead, two."

"So Flock and Cadenhead weren't necessarily working as a team," says De Villiers. "Flock moved in here. Killed Cadenhead and took over his life."

"Probably used their history to re-connect," says Susman. "May have groomed Cadenhead with drugs."

"Then killed him. Practised his carpentry skills on his body."

"Stepped right into his life," says Susman. "Wore his clothes, took his ID, used his credit card. Even had his fingerprints on ice if he ever needed to copy them."

"This takes 'identity theft' to a whole new level," says Breytenbach.

"Then, when the P.I. tracked the credit card statements and other paper trail details, he must have approached Flock."

Susman pulls away from the freezer which contains other bagged body parts. She drums her fingers on her crossed arms as she thinks. "He will kill again. He's looking for her head, now. Someone with dark hair, green eyes."

Khaya's in the doorway. "But how? How will he finish? Now that we have his ... monster. And he doesn't have any of his tools. He can't even use his M.O. as a delivery guy anymore."

"Flock doesn't know we've found this place yet. When he finds out, he'll be angry. But he'll see it as nothing more than a setback. He's clever and resourceful. He'll just start again. And I'll put money on the fact that he'll take someone else today. We need to warn them now."

"I'll call it in," says Khaya.

"Distribute the picture of his mother. He'll be looking for someone who looks like her. Any luck on finding his car yet?"

"He's in his own van. Or, at least, Cadenhead's van. They have circulated the registration details. High alert."

"Description of the vehicle?"

"Plain white panel van."

"We need to pull them over," says Susman. "Every one we see. Even if the plates don't match."

"I'll tell them."

"We need more hands on deck," says De Villiers. "Where is Vellie? And where the hell is Swanepoel?"

"Oh," says Breytenbach. "You haven't heard. He just got a call."

"Haven't heard what?"

"Swanepoel," says Breytenbach. "He's at the hospital. His mother died."

27

OXYGEN MASK

Susman's phone rings. She ignores it. She's busy watching CCTV footage of cars in all the places she thinks Flock could be. De Villiers is impatient, driven to the edge by clawing anxiety. He stares at Robin. "Are you going to get that?"

"Nah," she says, clicking on a new video. "Busy."

"Who is it?" he asks.

Distracted, she dismisses the question.

"Will you at least mute it, then? Or put your headphones on?"

"Oh, for God's sake," exclaims Susman. "It's my bloody therapist. She's determined, I'll give her that."

She answers the call and puts her earbuds in, with a pointed look at the detective. "Hello, Liz."

"Robin!" says her therapist. "Oh my. I've been trying to get you all day."

"Sorry. We've been under pressure here. In fact, I—"

"I was starting to worry," says Elizabeth.

Susman's mood is tinged with guilt. "Sorry, Liz."

"Now, you didn't call in for your session last night."

"I know. It's just been crazy here. We think we might have identified—"

"Listen, Robin. I know you're doing an essential job. I know that you're saving lives, okay? I don't take that lightly. I know you have minimal time and emotional bandwidth."

"Okay," says Susman.

"But we had an agreement. We are to have daily sessions while you are in Jo'burg. While you're on this job. We check in every day."

"I know. I just—"

"Robin, listen to me. You need to think self-preservation here. If you start spinning, you're not going to be able to help anyone. The police need your help, right?"

"Yes."

"They need you to be on top of your game, correct?"

"Yes."

"So you need to look after yourself. You need to check in with me. You need to take your pills. You need to talk it out. I don't care if you talk to me, or a friend, or your office plant. You need to process. You need to keep centred. Okay?"

Susman sighs. "You're right. I know you're right."

"Are you still meditating?" asks the therapist.

"Does lying in bed awake all night count?"

"No."

"Then ... no."

Susman was hoping for a laugh, but it's not the first time she thinks Elizabeth doesn't have much of a sense of humour.

"Do you need to talk about anything? Now, I mean?" asks Elizabeth. "I have twenty minutes."

"No. I—"

"I know. You need to go. But I'm here for you. Any time, okay? You can call me."

"Thanks, Liz. I appreciate it." Susman is about the end the call.

"Remember the oxygen mask," says the therapist.

"Yes," says Susman.

"Tell me about the oxygen mask."

Robin tries not to sigh. "If I'm on a plane and something goes wrong, and the oxygen masks drop, I need to put my own mask on before I can help others with their masks."

"Yes. You're no help to anyone if you're broken, Robin."

Unspoken words hang in the air. The soul-piercing truth is that she doesn't know how not to be broken.

"You're doing well," says Elizabeth. "You're keeping it together. It's almost over. Remember to check in with me. Talk. Take your pills. Breathe."

Susman hangs up and sighs; rubs her face.

"Coffee?" says De Villiers.

She looks at him as if she loves him. "Definitely. This waiting around is killing me. I want to be out there."

"We've got twenty vehicles on the lookout. They've got Flock's picture. They're pulling vans over. It's just a matter of time."

"I know. But he's out there. Stalking. Ready to pounce. I can feel it. I don't want ... I don't want any more bodies on my watch. And those babies. At night it's like I can hear them crying for their mothers. Mothers they'll never see again. Never remember. And there I lie in my hotel bed. Useless. And here I sit at the station. I'd rather be on the street, chasing down leads. It helps with the stress. To use the adrenaline, you know? Instead of having it eat you up from the inside. It's always been difficult for me to sit tight when there's someone out there."

"We're in the right place to co-ordinate," says De Villiers.

"I'd forgotten how hard this is."

"Let's get that coffee."

~

Lieutenant Swanepoel whacks Breytenbach on the shoulder, making him jump. "I'm going into Room Three to interview Mrs Sterling again. You game?"

"Swanepoel," Breytenbach looks concerned. "You shouldn't be working."

"Hey, this case isn't going to solve itself. Besides, I enjoy watching her squirm."

"You've just ... you've just lost your mother. You should be at home. With your family."

"I don't have any," says Swanepoel. "Not anymore."

"You should at least take some time off."

"It's easier. It's actually easier to work. Takes my mind off it."

"Okay," says Breytenbach. "Do what you need to do. But I want you to know that I've been there, you know? With my Dad. I know how it feels. Like a big part of you is missing. No matter how old you get, how independent, your parents are still your parents. It's a lifetime bond."

Swanepoel's eyes shine, and he looks uncomfortable.

"I'm here for you, brother," says Breytenbach. "Anything you need. I've got your back."

Swanepoel looks away. "Thanks, man."

"Oh, that reminds me. I have something for you." Breytenbach lifts the zip-up cooler bag on his desk and hands it to Swanepoel.

"Hey?"

"Lasagne," says Breytenbach. "When my Dad died, everyone showed up with food. Home-cooked meals. Things easy to freeze. It's just something our community does. My mom always said that it made her feel, like, supported. I was going to bring it over tonight, after the shift. But you're here, so—"

Swanepoel bites down and blinks his tears away.

"As you can see it's not exactly home-made," says Breytenbach. "But it's the best I could do while on duty."

"I wouldn't trust your home-made food anyway," says Swanepoel.

Breytenbach slaps Swanepoel on his back. "Now, are you ready to make that Mrs Sterling squirm?"

～

"Hello, Major," says the man they call *Smith*.

Major Alastair Denton looks up from his desk, concern knitting his brows. "What are you doing here?"

"I'm consulting with Narcotics. Totally legit."

The major stands up. "Well, come in and close the door before anyone sees you."

Smith closes the door. "I'm telling you, it's above board."

"It doesn't matter," says the major. "We should never be seen together. Ever."

"You're paranoid," says Smith.

"You're not paranoid enough."

They look at each other, waiting.

Finally, Smith talks. "I have news."

"I'm listening."

"The court action is still underway, but they'll rule soon. It's all happening quickly as if the gang have greased some palms. Story via the grapevine is that they will be released on early parole."

Denton grinds his teeth; his nostrils flare. "How?"

"I'm telling you, someone is paying. There is money passing hands here, under the table. I've heard that the Turbine Hall Gang has some serious capital."

"Well, it can't be allowed," says Alastair. "I won't let those thugs out on the street."

"Not much we can do about it, Major. It's the law."

"Well, sometimes the law needs a little help."

Smith laughs. "You're punking me, right? You're not serious."

The major's expression is serious.

"You're the squeakiest guy I know, Denton. You've never bent the law in your life."

"I need to know what you can do about the situation."

Smith shrugs. "Your wish is my command."

"I'd prefer it if it came from you."

"How convenient for you," says Smith. "You need to keep your hands clean. I get it."

"If, for some reason, you suddenly no longer like your job description, then—"

"All right, all right, I get it. You want to be able to sleep at night."

Blood rushes to the major's face. "I can't sleep at night! I can't sleep knowing that those psychopaths will get out, after what they've done!"

"Fine. I understand you don't want to give me a clear directive, but I need something."

"Like what?"

"Like ... do you want them ... to meet with an unfortunate accident in prison?"

"God. As much as I'd love to say yes, I can't. We can't be responsible for that."

"People die in prison all the time," says Smith. "We don't hear about them because society no longer cares. Criminals have lost their right to empathy. That gang? They've got plenty of enemies in there. I'm sure we can arrange for a guard to look the other way."

"No," says the major, shaking his head. "I won't have their blood on my hands."

"That's the beauty of it, Major. The blood would be on some other criminal's hands. Yours would be squeaky clean."

"Did you learn nothing from Macbeth?"

"I must have missed that class. Is this Shakespeare 101?" asks Smith. "Shall I sit down?"

"Don't you dare. You've been in here long enough."

Smith purses his lips. "So the gang gets to live."

"But they don't get to leave."

"Okay. I'll see what I can do."

"Smith," Alastair says as the man walks out. "Try to keep it within the bounds of the law."

Smith laughs and leaves the door open.

28

UNLUCKY IN LOVE

SWANEPOEL LEANS IN. "Mrs Sterling. Tell me about your affair with Ian Paviel."

The woman bristles. "We aren't having an affair. We're just friends. Ian runs the safari part of our business. We've known each other for years. It's a close relationship. It has to be!" As she crosses her arms, her bracelets clink and jingle. "We've been over this so many times. I'm exhausted. I've had enough. I'm going to go home."

"I wouldn't do that if I were you."

"Don't threaten my client, Lieutenant," says Sterling's lawyer.

"Me?" asks Swanepoel, feigning innocence. "Was I?"

"I won't let you intimidate Mrs Sterling. She's told you everything she knows. She's given you a signed statement. She couldn't have been more forthcoming."

Swanepoel doesn't hide his incredulity. "Forthcoming? Your client hasn't uttered a word of truth since she's been in here."

Annoyed, Sterling pouts and shakes back her platinum blonde hair.

The lawyer glares at Swanepoel. "I think it's time we leave."

"How do you explain your relationship history?" asks Breytenbach.

Sterling draws back, offended. "I beg your pardon?"

The lawyer sighs. "How is that relevant? It's beginning to sound like you lot are grasping at straws."

"Have you told him, yet, Barbs?" asks Swanepoel. "Have you told Mr Goldstein here that you're trailing in your wake no less than—" he counts on his fingers for effect. "Five dead husbands?"

The lawyer blinks as if he's just been slapped in the face.

"I've told him what I believe applies to the case. And as to my being unlucky in love—"

Swanepoel laughs out loud. "Unlucky in love? This isn't a rom-com on the bloody silver screen."

"More like a crime thriller," says Breytenbach.

She narrows her eyes at him. "I do hope you're not suggesting—"

"Mrs Sterling. Or shall I call you Mrs Hopkins? Or Mrs Sigalas, or Mrs Peterson?"

"Enough!" roars the woman. "That's enough! I won't have you—"

The lawyer's face is pinched. "I think it would be in your best interests to not say another word."

Swanepoel shrugs at Mrs Sterling. "You don't have to cooperate. It's your funeral."

"Actually," says Swanepoel. "It's her husband's funeral. Her fifth husband's funeral."

"Look at me!" yells the woman. "Look at the size of me. I weigh 52 kilograms!"

"Mazel tov," says Swanepoel. "What's your point?"

Her lawyer reiterates his legal advice. "I suggest you say nothing further, Mrs Sterling."

"My husband weighed over 90 kilograms. My point is that I wouldn't have the strength to do what was done to him."

"Oh," says Breytenbach. "I wasn't for a moment suggesting that you did the deed yourself. People like you—"

"People *like me?*" sneers Sterling.

"People like you don't like to get your hands dirty. I wouldn't expect you to do so much as to make your own bed, never mind kill your own husband."

"Is this what this ridiculous interrogation is about? You don't like wealthy people? You feel hard done by? Let me guess ... if my people hadn't oppressed your people during Apartheid, then you'd be a tycoon on a yacht somewhere instead of in this hole of a police station. Well, let me tell you that without *people like me*, people like you wouldn't have jobs. Or our tax money."

Breytenbach lets her words hang in the air, bitter and lonely. "Who did you get to kill your husband, Mrs Sterling?"

She simmers quietly. "I'm quite sure I don't know what you are talking about."

"That's funny," says Swanepoel. "That's funny, Breytenbach, isn't it?"

"Yep," says Breytenbach. He's not smiling.

"Because we tracked your boyfriend down and he doesn't seem to agree with your version of events."

She's about to say something but closes her mouth—a gaping silver fish.

"You're looking a bit pale, Mrs Hopkins. I mean, Mrs Sterling."

"Paviel's in the room next door," says Swanepoel. "And he seemed quite ... annoyed when we told him your version of events."

"Annoyed," agrees Breytenbach, nodding. "Agitated. He was pretty pissed off, to be honest."

"What are you talking about? I never said anything about Ian. This has nothing to do with him!"

"Ah, well, it might have been because we tweaked your story a bit."

"What do you mean?" she looks at her lawyer. "Ira, what do they mean? Are they allowed to do that?"

Goldstein is antsy. "What are you two getting at?"

"We may have hinted to Paviel that Barbs here pinned the blame on him."

"No," says Sterling, eyes wide despite the Botox freezing her forehead.

"He wasn't happy," says Swanepoel, feigning concern.

"In fact, he completely changed his story. From not knowing anything to knowing exactly what happened to the deceased."

"You're bluffing," says the lawyer, loosening his tie. "They're bluffing. Don't listen to them."

"He told us everything. Every detail. And do you know what? His story checks out. He told us where you bought the rope from. The tape. He showed us the bag you transported the body in. We've corroborated every detail. It all checks out."

"Every detail," says Breytenbach.

"You thought you could do it together. You were in love. You were a team. Bonny and Clyde."

Breytenbach, unblinking, holds Mrs Sterling's gaze. "Paviel is in serious debt. He's about to lose all his assets. Richard Sterling had more money than he knew what to do with, and you are the sole bene-ficiary."

"You convinced Paviel to kill your husband so that the two of you could live happily ever after."

"Or, at least, until you become *Mrs* Paviel," says Breytenbach. "And then he would have to watch his back."

"I think that's what surprised Paviel most, you know."

Mrs Sterling grits her teeth and stares at Swanepoel.

"He was pretty shocked when we told him about your habit of, well ... knocking off husbands. It all came spilling out once we showed him the wedding photos."

Breytenbach nods. "And the death certificates."

"We couldn't shut him up, after that. No detail was too small."

"That bastard," she says. "That bloody traitorous bastard!"

"Please, Mrs Sterling," cautions the lawyer. "Not another word."

"He doesn't deserve your loyalty," says Swanepoel.

Breytenbach nods. "He dished on you like a steak at dinner-time."

The lawyer stands up, flustered. "Look, I've had enough. We are no longer cooperating with you. Let us go, or charge my client with something."

"We'd be more than happy to charge Mrs Sterling," says Swanepoel. "Our question is, does she have anything to say to mitigate the charges against her? She's looking at premeditated murder for this, and who knows what else we'll find when we go digging around in her past. She's looking at decades of hard time. Have you seen the condition of our prisons? There's no Rich Women's Wing. On a good day, there is running water and cutlery. But that doesn't matter, really, because I don't think she'll last a day."

"I'm not going to prison," she says.

Breytenbach nods. "If you'd like to change your story—perhaps the judge will go easier on you—the time is now."

The lawyer looks more nervous than ever. "Barbara. Don't do anything rash. They're manipulating you. It's a clumsy attempt at getting you to—"

"Okay," she says to the officers, eyes like arctic lasers. Then she looks down at her hands on the table; a gesture of defeat.

"Not another word, Barbara," says the lawyer. His hands are pulsing at his sides as if he wants to duct tape his client's mouth. "Think about what you're doing."

"What's there to think about?" she demands. "I'm not going to prison!"

The lawyer slumps down again and sinks his head in his hands.

Still staring down, she mumbles something.

"What was that?" asks Breytenbach.

She looks up at him slowly. Her face is an iceberg. "I'll tell you everything."

29

ROSEBANK HEIGHTS

THE ECN CAMERAMAN stands at the foot of the Rosebank Heights block of flats, camera trained on Jennifer Walker. She's wearing her Go-Get-'Em outfit: skinny black jeans, stylish leather jacket, and stilettos that match her crimson lipstick. She has sneakers in the car in case she has to literally go get anybody.

"Three, two—" says the cameraman.

"Wait," says Walker. "How's my hair?"

"Hair? Fine."

"Just fine?"

"*Ja*," says the man. "It's fine."

"One day someone will teach you the art of the compliment," says Walker.

"I doubt it. Can I roll?"

She nods.

He holds three fingers in the air. *Three, two, one.*

Jennifer Walker clears her throat and looks into the camera. "Who would have guessed that in this upmarket neighbourhood—Rosebank, known for its tree-lined avenues, fashion, shopping, restaurants and tourist attractions—lurks the darkest of evils. At ten o'clock this morning the police raided what they believed to be the residence of the Jigsaw Killer. The evidence they found has been described as grotesque and damning. Sources close to the investigating unit said that Flock's apartment was 'a scene out of a horror movie'. Body parts of no less than seven victims were discovered, five of them female: Sandra Longman; Desiree Van Zyl; Emily Shuter; Denise Metlerkamp, and Carey Bosman. Bosman was reported missing from her Linden home only yesterday morning. Detective De Villiers of the Parkview Police informed all news agents today that they have identified the killer as 'David Flock' who may operate under the name—the stolen identity—of Zachary Cadenhead. Flock's picture, on screen now, has been widely circulated, and the police are urging the public to call in if they have any information. There is a dedicated call centre to receive tip-offs: the number is on screen now. Flock's vehicle is described as a plain white panel van, and his modus operandi has in the past involved posing as a courier—a delivery man—for an online baby product company in the Parks area. The victims to date have all been brunettes with small babies. David Flock should be regarded as armed and dangerous. The SAP would like to appeal to the public to remain calm but cautious and to call in if they have any information regarding the case. Stay safe, and keep your eyes peeled. This is Jennifer Walker, reporting for ECN."

The cameraman stops filming and nods. "I'll upload it now. That was good."

"Really?" says Walker, squinting at him, holding onto a nearby pole for balance as she adjusts one of her high heels.

"A good balance of emotion and information."

"Hell, I may have been wrong about you," she teases. She helps him pack up his kit, and they load the car.

"Where to now?" he asks. "We gonna get a word with that Sterling woman?"

"It's a great story. Plastic surgery, safaris, sex, betrayal, money, murder..."

"It's got everything."

"Let's hold off. We'll get to her later."

"Seriously? The ruthlessly ambitious Jennifer Walker has something better to do than to chase one of the sexiest stories of the year?"

"I want to be on the streets. I want to stop Flock. And not just for the story. I want him off the streets."

He looks aghast. "Um, what? You want to look for *a serial killer*?"

"Well, he's around, isn't he? This is his neighbourhood. We may as well drive around for a bit and look for him."

He frowns at her as they climb into the car. "Okay."

"Okay, you agree?"

"Okay, I'll do it. As long as you're not going to do anything crazy."

"Me?" says Jennifer, making loony eyes at him. "Do something crazy?"

"Yes, Walker. Crazy. Like when you dragged me along to that *tik* warehouse, and we almost got blasted full of hollow points."

"That was just bad luck," she says. "Or ... good luck, if you remember that we didn't get shot."

He shakes his head and starts the car. "So you kept saying. So you say every time you get us into hot water."

Walker sighs and looks out of the window. "Sometimes I think you'd be more suited to being a D.O.P."

"Oh, come on. Just because I have a family to support and I don't want to die young—"

"Seriously. You should be shooting, like, homemakers talking about the latest in stain removal. Or kids eating cereal. Or tampon ads. Not a lot of fatalities in that line of work, I believe."

"A job in advertising would pay a lot better than this gig," he agrees.

"You'd die of boredom. Also, how would you handle waking up every morning to face a day that doesn't involve me?"

"That sounds absolutely bloody wonderful."

She hits him on the shoulder.

"Ouch!" he says. "That's a mean right hook you've got there, Walker."

"My instinct is telling me we should be out here, looking. We're just going to drive around with our eyes open," she says.

"As opposed to ... driving around with our eyes shut?"

"Don't be nervous. It's not like I'm going to get a baby and act as bait or anything."

"Get a baby? Just the fact that idea even occurred to you scares the pants off me," he says.

"Well, it's a great idea."

"Bat-shit crazy," mutters the cameraman. "Where would you *get a baby*, anyway?" When she's about to reply, he stops her by putting up his hand. "Never mind. I don't want to know."

30

CONTRABAND

Devil ends the call and closes his eyes, trying to pull himself together. Breytenbach and Swanepoel stride into the station.

"Hey, Devil," says Swanepoel. "We just walked past the dedicated phone line for Jigsaw tip-offs, and it's going insane."

De Villiers blinks at them, tries to orient himself to where he is in time and space instead of thinking of his missing son. Of when he taught Niel to tie his shoelaces; make a sandwich; catch a fish. The one night he'll always remember—when he hugged the five-year-old goodnight, and the boy had whispered in his ear—*I wish this would never end.* After that, the steamtrain of adolescence swept along, catching them all off-guard. Girls. Independence. Graduation. It all happened so quickly. And all of that for what? Now they're pulling bodies out of the kibbutz ruins, and De Villiers doesn't even know if his son is alive or dead.

He takes a sharp breath and looks at the lieutenants. "Good," he says. "Good. Hopefully, we'll be able to find something somewhere in the avalanche. Look, Swanepoel, about your mother. I know you said earlier that you don't want to go home, that you'd rather be working—"

"That's right. And it's a good thing, too, because Breyts and I just cracked the Sterling case wide open."

"Tell me?"

"Swanepoel was on form," says Breytenbach. "It was a beautiful thing to behold."

Swanepoel grins. "Breytenbach was also ... not shit."

"Details?"

"So, despite having her lawyer in the room, Mrs Sterling confessed to manipulating Paviel—her lover—into killing her husband. Mr Sterling was getting suspicious of their relationship, threatened to leave her, take his money."

"Paviel has lost all his wealth and more, gambling online. Doesn't have two cents of his own to rub together."

Swanepoel unwraps a sandwich. "Mrs Sterling was funding his life-style. If Mr Sterling left her, they'd have nothing."

"And now they have a lot less than nothing," says Breytenbach.

"Have you found him yet?" asks Devil. "Paviel?"

"No, but don't tell Mrs Sterling that! He won't go far. He's green and broke. He'll show up somewhere."

"He'll turn himself in. A man like that, coerced into killing. He'll come in, come clean, and blame it all on Sterling."

"Well, it was her idea," says Swanepoel.

"But he was stupid enough to go through with it."

"He won't think it was *her* idea," says De Villiers. "Master manipulators like her plant an idea in your head so subtly that you end up thinking it was your idea."

"I thought all women did that," says Swanepoel.

"Watch it, Swanepoel," comes Susman's voice from a chair that swivels to face him.

"Oops," he says, looking sheepish. "Sorry. Didn't see you there."

"That's no excuse," says Robin.

Swanepoel changes the topic swiftly. "Where are we on Flock?"

"We're so close," says Susman. "It's driving us crazy, sitting here."

"*Fokkit*," says De Villiers. "Maybe it's time to get out there."

Susman jumps up. "I'm game."

"Me too," says Khaya. "This chair is burning a hole in my arse."

Susman laughs, and Khaya shoots her a puzzled look.

"What?"

"You have a very endearing way of mixing your metaphors, Khaya. That was an especially good one. I'm going to start using it."

The phone in her pocket buzzes; she pulls it out.

"*Gah*," she says. "I'm still not used to this thing."

"Your phone?" asks De Villiers.

"On the farm, I have a landline. It's one of those old exchanges—you have to rotary-dial through to the operator to place a call. Sometimes you can listen in to your neighbours' conversations. Pick up the local gossip."

"'That's something you can't do with texting," says De Villiers.

"Exactly." She reads the text and frowns.

"Bad news?" asks the detective.

"I don't know. It's from an unknown number."

"Let me guess. You've won the Nigerian lottery? Or it's one of your pet sheep, asking you to come home?"

Susman ignores De Villiers' attempt at a quip. "It says to turn on the news. Channel 128."

Swanepoel crosses the room and changes the television channel to 128, then turns the volume up.

The news anchor reads in a neutral accent. "In breaking news: Judge Mbete of the North Gauteng High Court in Pretoria has rescinded her decision to grant the infamous Turbine Hall Gang early parole. They reportedly found the gang with contraband in their prison cells in a random search today. Cell phones, marijuana cigarettes, alcohol, and a hand-fashioned weapon were discovered."

A cheer goes up in the police station.

"Not only was Mbete's decision rescinded, but there will be new charges laid against the gang, charges that, if the men are convicted, may double their sentences."

There is another cheer, this time it's louder. A few of the officers steal discreet glances at Susman, and she feels the heat in her cheeks, but more obvious is her feeling of utter relief.

"The crowd greeted this news with jubilation outside the courts just a moment ago." The video clip on screen is now of the protestors outside the courthouse celebrating: dancing, ululating. "The gathering who were protesting the convicts' early release are now celebrating their unexpected victory."

They hold their banners and placards high, many emblazoned with the photographs of the gang's victims, including the fifteen-year-old Themba Xeke.

"Xeke was shot while attempting to protect his mother, who also lost her life at the hands of the gang. This is clearly a welcome turn of events that is a balm to a crowd still angry over the Turbine Hall Gang's originally lean sentence."

They move on to the next story, and Swanepoel lowers the volume again. "Contraband? How fortuitous. That's good news if I've ever heard it."

"Yes," says Susman.

De Villiers eyes her suspiciously. "But you don't look surprised."

"That's because I'm not."

His eyes grow wide. "Susman. You didn't."

"I didn't what?"

"Did you ... did you arrange for those things to be planted in their cells?"

She pauses. "No."

"*Jussis*. You did. I can see it on your face. Don't get me wrong; I think it was genius—"

"This is merely the face of a relieved woman, De Villiers."

"You're a *fokken* genius, Susman. End of story."

Susman looks amused. "It wasn't me."

"Ha," laughs De Villiers. "That's what they said."

31

THIS IS THE ONLY COPY

SWANEPOEL AND BREYTENBACH RIDE TOGETHER. They slam their doors shut, and when Swanepoel puts his key in the ignition, the CD player screams Nickelback at them. He turns it off.

"Hey, Swanepoel," says Breytenbach.

"*Ja?*"

"You okay?"

"*Ja.*"

"Is there ... is there anything I can do for you? Help you organise the funeral?"

"No. Thanks."

"I could take over something small for you if you like. Organise the—I don't know—the flowers or something. Or the cakes."

"Cakes? What do you know about cakes? You going to start baking when you get home?"

"Don't joke," says Breytenbach. "I have an aunty that is an excellent baker."

"Listen," says Swanepoel. His face is dark. "Something came in for you. At the station."

"What was it? From who?"

"I don't know. It looked personal, so I didn't want to leave it on your desk. It's in my case, there. You can open it."

Breytenbach snaps open Swanepoel's bag and retrieves a padded envelope. "This?"

Swanepoel's eyes flick down to the parcel. "*Ja.*"

"Why do you have it?"

"I told you. Someone dropped it off at the station, and I didn't want to leave it on your desk."

Breytenbach frowns. "When?"

"I don't know ... it's been such a crazy day. Sometime this morning?"

Breytenbach leaves it on his lap, eyeing it suspiciously.

Swanepoel glances at him. "You don't have any enemies, do you?"

"What do you mean?"

"You know, jilted lovers, political rivals, religious fundamentalists?"

"No," says Breytenbach. "Why do you ask?"

"That package doesn't have a return address, and you don't know who sent it. Don't take this the wrong way, buddy, but if you have any enemies, I don't want you opening that thing in my car."

"Hey?"

"Damn it, Breytenbach. Where's your sense of self-preservation? What if there is anthrax in there? Or if it's a letter bomb? Don't you watch any spy thrillers on TV?"

"But I'm a *lekker* guy. Who would want to kill me?"

"I don't know, Breytenbach. That's a very good question."

Breytenbach laughs. "You're paranoid, you know that?"

"Paranoid people live longer."

"It's probably nothing," says Breytenbach. "It's probably a Christmas card."

"In July?"

"SAPO have been on strike for months. I wouldn't be surprised."

"It was hand-delivered," says Swanepoel. "I don't want you opening that thing in my car."

"Swanepoel, if you really thought it was a letter bomb there's no way you would've put it in your bag."

"Maybe, maybe not. Maybe when I put it in there, I was in a different mood. Maybe I didn't mind the idea of being blown to smithereens."

Breytenbach considers that. "Do you believe in, you know, heaven?"

"Ja," says Swanepoel. "I think so. I hope so."

Breytenbach opens the envelope.

"Hey!" exclaims Swanepoel. "What are you doing?"

"What do you think? I'm opening it."

Swanepoel bangs the steering wheel and shifts in his seat. "What do you know? I get to share a car with Erol 'Deathwish' Breytenbach."

"There we go," says the lieutenant. "And look. We're still alive."

"For now," says Swanepoel, glancing down. "What is it?"

Breytenbach empties the padded envelope onto his lap. A CD in a jewel case and a note fall out.

"Okay. Well, thanks for not blowing us up."

Breytenbach holds up the note. It says in capital letters THIS IS THE ONLY COPY.

"What the hell does that mean?" asks Swanepoel.

Breytenbach leans back into the car seat and sighs. Then he looks at the roof of the car as if he is thanking a higher power. "It doesn't matter," he says. "It's over. That's all that matters."

They travel in silence for a while, then Breytenbach murmurs something.

"What's that?" asks Swanepoel.

"I just said *thank you*."

"Me? For what?" asks the lieutenant.

"You know what. Thank you for the package."

An intense silence crowds the interior of the car. Finally, Swanepoel looks contrite. "Look, Breytenbach," he says. "I'm sorry, okay? I'll pay you back. I was desperate for the money. For my mother."

"I know," says Breytenbach.

"Just give me some time," says Swanepoel. "I promise I'll pay it all back." Swanepoel is quiet for a while, then continues. "And I want you to know that your secret is safe with me. I'll never tell anyone about what's on that video."

"I shouldn't have to keep it a secret," says Breytenbach. "It's not like I'm doing anything wrong. I'm not ashamed of it, you know? I just know that if people know I'm gay, my job as a cop will be a lot harder."

Swanepoel shrugs. "You're right. I wish you weren't."

32

GLITTER IN THE DUSK

VERITY PARK PLAYGROUND, **Parkhurst, 17th of July 2014, 16:35.**

A blonde woman sits on a park bench, watching the sun sink. The sky is ablaze with orange, and the breeze wicks the warmth from her cheeks. She's singing a song to her baby boy, who is tucked up in his pram, cooing back at her.

"*1, 2, 3, 4, 5, once I caught a fish alive. 6, 7, 8, 9, 10, then I let him go again. Why did you let him go? 'Cos he bit my finger so. Which finger did he bite? This little finger on my right.*"

Sarah is exhausted from months of sleep deprivation and the relentless demands of being a new mother. Despite the constant fug in her head, when she looks at her son, she feels a deep connection; a quiet joy she's never experienced before. He coos again, and she laughs. "You like that song, baba. You like it. Yes! Have you had enough now? Shall we go home? Let's pack up this picnic blanket."

She tosses the baby toys into the bag and shakes the blanket out, folds it, packs it into the bottom of the pram. The baby babbles.

"Yes," she replies. "I think so, too. It's late! It will be dark soon! All the other babies have gone home. They're having their baths already. Or maybe their dinners. We must get a move-on!"

She pushes the pram, fighting the resistance the thick grass offers the wheels. It's later than she thought. Darker than she expected. She scolds herself for losing track of time, which she does at least once a day since she's become this mom-zombie version of herself. She opens the bent pedestrian gate, clicking it closed behind her. The sign instructing dog handlers to clean up after their pets is hanging askew; has been for months. All it needs is a cable-tie, she thinks every time she sees it, but never remembers to bring one.

Sarah's startled by a gasp a few meters ahead of her on the sidewalk. She watches as a young man trips over a loose paver and tips forward. He falls hard. His long limbs splay out over the potholed pavement; he exclaims in pain and cradles his arm. Sarah's grip increases on the handle of the pram as she rushes to him, shocked. "Oh, my goodness! Are you okay?"

He groans but is able to stand.

"That was quite a fall," says Sarah. "Oh, dear, you're bleeding!"

"Ah. I think I broke my arm," says the man. His dark eyes glitter in the dusk.

"You're hurt. What can I do? Shall I drive you to a hospital?"

"No, no." He shakes his head. "I live just around the corner. And you have your baby to think about."

"I can arrange for someone to drive you? I'll call a cab. Or an ambulance."

"No, I'll be fine. Really." He leans against the trunk of an oak tree. "I'm seeing stars. I just need a minute. I'll be okay."

"Here," says Sarah. "Sugar. For the shock." She grabs a juice box from the baby bag and rips the straw off the back with her teeth, then punctures the foil with it. The baby is fighting sleep, and Sarah wants to get him home and fed before he succumbs.

The man thanks her and gulps down the juice. "I have to get home. My wife is expecting me."

"Let's phone her. Maybe she can collect you?"

"Yes," says Flock. "We live just up the road."

Sarah gets her phone out. It's getting darker by the moment, and she wants to get home now. "What's her number?"

The baby grizzles. He'll be crying soon.

"Shush, baba. Shhh. We'll be home soon. You'll be snug in your bed before you know it." Phone in hand, she turns back to the man. "What's your wife's number?"

"Oh dear," he says, raising his hand to his forehead. "My mind's gone blank. I think I might have hit my head harder than I thought."

He has a small scar under his eye which shines under the light of the streetlamp. Sarah looks up and down the street, hoping to find someone else who can help.

"My phone is in my car," says the man. "It's just here. I have her on speed-dial."

"I'll help you get over there," Sarah says. "Hold my arm."

They trundle over to the white panel van.

"Thank you," he says, looking at her intently. "You are very kind."

"It's nothing," says Sarah. If she leaves now, she'll get home just before dark.

"I can see you're a very good mother." He stops and searches his pocket for his key, then unlocks the van. The vehicle lights flicker. "I keep my phone in the back," he says. "So it doesn't get stolen."

Sarah's instinct is to leave immediately. There's something about the man that's unnerving.

"You can never be too cautious," he says. He opens the rear passenger door. "It's just under the back seat there, would you mind? I don't think I can lean in without—"

"I don't see it," says Sarah. "Sorry. I have to get home." The baby whimpers. She holds his small hand to comfort him, and when she looks back at the man, he forces a white pad up to her face, pressing it over her nose and mouth. She's never smelt chloroform before, but she knows that's what it is. She lets go of the pram and tries to fight him, tries to kick him, scratch him, smash his nose, but instead, her body wilts into his, and her mind fades to static.

~

The baby screams and screams into the night. A woman, walking home from work, hears the boy and rushes up to the pram.

"Hello, baby? Hello, little one. Hey? What's going on here? Where's your mommy?" She looks around, but can't see anyone. "Hello? Hello anybody? There's a baby here! Hello?"

The night does not reply.

"I'm going to pick you up. If your mommy comes back, she'll be cross with me, but shame. You're crying, hey. Poor baby. Come to Nancy."

She lifts him from the pram and tries to comfort him. Rocks him, shushes him. She can tell he's exhausted from crying, and his hands are cold.

"Come, come, come," she says. "There we go. Hello, boo-boo. Hello la-la. Where's your mommy? What am I going to do with you? *Hai* man. Baby, you want to come home to Nancy's house in Diepsloot? You sleep in Nancy's bed?"

A security company patrol car turns the corner and heads her way. She jumps and waves at them to stop. "Hey! Hey *'mfowethu*. Stop!"

The guard rolls down his window. "*Sisi?*"

She hears the beeping of their radio system inside the car.

"There's a problem here," says the nanny. "There's a big problem here. We need to call the police."

33

DUSK

"DEVIL HERE," says the detective. "I'm driving. You're on speakerphone."

"He's taken another one," says Khaya.

Susman feels like punching the dashboard.

"Where?" asks De Villiers. "What happened?"

"A security patrol car just called in an abandoned baby in Parkhurst."

"Who is she?"

"They don't know yet. There was no identification in the pram."

"Pram?"

"She was abducted from the park. From the playground."

"That's not Flock's M.O.," says the detective. "How do we know it was him?"

"He's desperate," says Susman. "He can't use the delivery ruse anymore. He has to snatch them somehow."

He shakes his head. "I don't like this."

"Khaya," says Susman. "Anyone reported her missing, yet?"

"No. It only happened, like, half an hour ago. A nanny found the baby —someone else's nanny—she was on her way home, and she came across a pram at the park. She flagged down the patrol car. Her story checks out. She's here, at the station. She didn't know about the Jigsaw Killer. She's distraught."

"She could have seen something," says Susman.

"I don't know what else to ask her," says Khaya. "I've asked her everything. She's crying. She won't talk any more. She keeps asking for the baby."

"Keep going," says De Villiers. "Make her a strong cup of tea and explain that she can help us find the baby's mother. Make her remember."

"I think Flock was gone when she got there. It was dusk when she found him."

"Have you shown her Flock's picture?" asks Susman.

"Yes. She didn't see anyone like that. She said the park was deserted by the time she got to it. She was late. She was running for a taxi."

"No cars?"

"No cars."

"Damn it," says De Villiers. "Canvas the street. Maybe a neighbour saw something."

He ends the call and grinds his teeth. "DAMN IT!"

"I'm also angry," says Susman. "Frustrated. But we need calm and focus. As we speak, Flock is driving around with this woman in his van."

"Don't speak to me like a child," says De Villiers.

"I'm sorry. But I need you on this. I need the whole man, the whole detective that is De Villiers on this case with me right now."

"I am!" he yells. "What do you think I'm doing? I'm right here!"

"André. Remember when you dragged me away from my farm. You told me that we were the only people who could stop this guy, who can stop him from taking mothers away from their babies." She stops to take a breath. "Now, I know you're worried to death about Niel."

De Villiers' knuckles are white on the steering wheel.

"And I know you want to save this baby's mother. We've almost got him. I can feel it. We're close, André, we're so close I can practically smell his breath. But we've got this small window in time to act, and there is no margin for error."

"Yes," says De Villiers. He forces his hunched-up shoulders down and opens his window for fresh air. "I'm sorry. I just ... I just saw red. My blood boiled."

"It's normal," says Susman. "You're human. You're under a lot of stress. I'm angry as all hell."

"I wanted to stop him before he took someone else."

"It's not too late," says Susman. "We can still save her."

34

A REAL MOTHER

THE WHITE PANEL van is speeding along the highway. The driver is manic, swerving and lane-switching. Ear-splitting death metal reverberates through the cabin, and he shouts the lyrics and bangs the steering wheel with the heel of his palm. Sarah groans from the back seat and covers her face, trying to fight off the man with chloroform, not realising it is too late. Her head is pounding; her mouth is dry. She forces herself to sit up, and the world is spinning.

David Flock notices her waking up and turns the music down. "Ah! She's awake! Well, thank you for joining us, Mother! It's about time!"

Sarah frowns at him, trying to put the pieces together. Her thoughts are slow and confusing.

It was getting dark.

The man fell.

Where is Matthew?

"Just lie back, relax," says Flock. "Put your feet up! We're almost there."

"What happened?" Panic claws at her throat. "Where's my baby?"

"There's nothing to worry about, Mother. I've been good. I've taken care of everything."

Fear shreds her voice. "What do you mean? What do you mean you've taken care of everything? Where is my baby?"

"You're worried. It's understandable."

"Is he here? Is he in the car? Matthew?"

"There's no need to scream. Screaming won't change anything."

Suddenly, she catches sight of his troubled eyes in the rear-view mirror and freezes. Her body goes stiff with fear; her organs melt. "No," she says. "No. Oh, my God. You're him."

Flock shoots her a look that she can't read.

"You're him. The killer, on the news."

"I told you I'd be on TV one day. You always said I was worth nothing. Less than nothing. Now, look! Everyone knows about me." He takes his hands off the steering wheel and gestures victoriously. "I'm famous!"

Sarah scrambles to think past the panic that's painting her brain numb. She can't die. Matthew can't grow up without a mother, not when she's got so much love to give. There's no time to waste; she needs to switch to survival mode. She has to forget about Matthew for long enough to save her own life because when she experiences this scary empty-armed feeling it erodes her logic. There is no Matthew. There is no Sarah. It's just her body playing a part to survive.

"You're … famous," she ventures. "Everyone knows about you."

"I always knew I would be," he says, his hands still in the air.

"Everyone is talking about you," says Sarah.

Flock's van drifts into the next lane, causing the car alongside them to caution him by hooting. Flock gets angry and shouts at the driver, swearing at him, waving his fist around like a lunatic. Then he grabs the wheel decisively and speeds up.

"They're taking me seriously now," says Flock, ignoring the dashboard that is lit up with warnings. He's revving too high; he's driving too fast.

"Not like before," says Sarah.

"Before, no one listened to me. When I told them about you. About how you used to hurt me. No one cared."

"Your mom," says Sarah carefully, "used to hurt you?"

"Don't act as if you don't know that. Don't act as if you don't know!"

"I didn't mean it," she says. "I didn't mean it as a question. I do know."

"You're just like them," he says, bitterness in every word.

"I'm not. I'm not. I care about what happened to you. No mother should ever hurt her child. Never. It should never happen."

"They say, 'Tell someone!' 'Tell someone!' but then you tell someone and no one does anything about it. Then Mother finds out you've been titty-taling and then you get locked in the bathroom cupboard for a week." He grimaces. "Mom used to call it titty-taling."

"Tattle-taling?"

"Vulgar. Always so vulgar. Not like a Real Mother should be."

"How should a ... a real mother be?"

"A Real Mother is pure of spirit. Virtuous. A Real Mother radiates love and forgiveness. She's a lady. She wears clean underwear. She doesn't have dirty boyfriends. She doesn't make you lie in her stained bed with her. She doesn't hold you under until you suffocate."

"She used to lock you in ... a cupboard?"

"It was dark and dark was scary, but it didn't matter anyway because my eyes were swollen shut."

"She hit you?"

"No one listened. No one cared."

"I ... I bet that if you called the news channel, they'd put you on air. You could talk to the whole country. Tell them everything. They'll all listen to you now. Everyone cares about you now."

"They would!" he laughs. "They would."

"Why don't we ... stop. Stop the car and make the call?"

Flock laughs again. "Stop? No, we're not stopping, Mommy."

The hair on the back of her neck stands up when he calls her that. She feels like vomiting.

"We have no time to stop. We're speeding ahead! We're speeding right into the jaws of our destiny."

35

THE BAD OLD DAYS

NORTH GAUTENG HIGH COURT, **17th of July 2014, 17:08.**

Smith stands outside the court building, fidgeting with the file in his hands while he waits for the major to answer his call. There is a flurry of activity around him, including sirens approaching and retreating — police tape flitters in the breeze. Third time lucky; he finally hears the call connect.

"Denton," he says, out of breath. "We have a serious problem."

"Smith!" sings the major. "Nothing you say can dampen my spirits. You did such an excellent job on the Turbine Hall Gang."

"That's what I'm calling about," says Smith.

"I was just about to say that you can expect a large bonus coming your way. Best news I've had in—"

"They're out, Major. They're out."

"*Out?* What do you mean they're *out?* I've just heard on the news that they'll get additional time added to their sentences."

"It was a ploy. The whole thing was a bloody ploy—"

The major pauses. "What was?"

"The motion for early parole. They never thought they'd actually get it."

"What?"

"The court proceedings ... it was just a way to get out of prison, to get into a car. There was a shoot-out."

Alastair blinks. "You're not making any sense."

"There are three officers down. They attacked the vehicle transporting the gang back to the prison."

"What?!"

"I told you they had support outside. I knew it!"

"Where are they now? The gang?"

"Two of them are dead. I can see their bodies from here."

"And the other three?"

"Long gone."

"The leader? Mabaleng?" asks the major. The most dangerous one.

"Gone."

Alastair feels the urge to throw his phone against the wall and see it shatter into a thousand pieces.

"How?" he demands. "How could this have happened?"

"I don't know what to tell you. They jumped the car like professionals. Like goddamn soldiers. I haven't seen anything like it since the bad old days. It all happened in less than a minute. Teargas. Gunshots. Bleeders on the ground. And then they were gone."

Alastair needs his phone in good working order, so he kicks his wastepaper bin across the room instead. His jaws ache with fury.

"Major?" asks Smith.

"Keep me informed."

"Yes, Sir. Would you like me to do anything else? I mean, other than keep you up to date?"

"Don't tempt me, Smith."

"I have some men. A team. Good at gathering intel. Good at making people ... disappear. We can try to track Mabaleng down. The team's expensive, but they're worth it. Just say the word."

"If it got out ... it would be the end of my career."

"If the Turbine Hall Gang gets hold of Susman ... it'll be the end of her. Full stop."

"You're right," he says. "Do it."

"Do it?" asks Smith. "You're sure? These aren't the kind of guys you can pull off once they're on the job. No second thoughts. No going back. Final is final."

The major's mind is made up. "Do it," he says.

36

DOUBLE BINGO

SWANEPOEL AND BREYTENBACH CRUISE AROUND, listening to their police radio for developments. After Swanepoel's confession, they're in a quiet, contemplative mood.

"It's getting dark," says Breytenbach, breaking the silence between them. "I don't like searching for killers in the dark."

Swanepoel looks across at him, then back at the road. "My mom ... when I was small and scared, my mom used to say that being afraid of the dark is like being afraid of nothing. Because darkness is absence. Darkness is nothing. So, then she used to say: if you're afraid of nothing, you're actually very brave."

"Hm," says Breytenbach. "My mom just used Monster Spray."

"Hey?"

"You know. Monster Spray. She'd take an empty spray bottle, like an old Windolene bottle, and put some monster stickers on it. Fill it with tap water and spray in our cupboards and under our beds. It kept the monsters away."

Swanepoel's phone rings. "Hello, Sweet Lips. I'm driving. Can I call you back later?"

"Don't you dare put the phone down," says Jennifer Walker. "I've just received a tip-off. I think it's good."

"What?" he almost drops the phone.

"On the Jigsaw case," she says.

"How do you know it's good?" asks Swanepoel.

"It wasn't from an anonymous caller or anything. It was from a retired journo who thinks he may have spotted Flock. Said it looked just like him and he was driving a nondescript white van."

"Holy shit!"

"It was dark already—it happened, like, five minutes ago—and the vehicle license plates had been removed. Said he tried to get the guy's attention, to see if it was him."

"He approached him?"

"Well, they were both on the highway. He first noticed the guy because his driving was all over the place. So he hooted and made a nuisance of himself. Said the guy went crazy. Super aggressive, almost ran him off the road, then lost him. That's when he called me. He had my number, knew I was working on the case. Asked me to call the cops. I'll phone the station now; I just wanted to let you know first."

"Which highway?"

"The M1 South. M for Mike."

"Got it." Swanepoel puts his foot down.

"It happened near Empire road. He didn't take the off-ramp."

"Walker. I could kiss you."

She laughs. "You'd better!"

"I'll call you later. Give you an exclusive."

"Is that what they're calling it nowadays?"

"Haha."

"Just remember to bring your *prowess*."

"You're hilarious," he says. "Hell, I like you."

Walker hesitates. "Stay alive, if at all possible."

"I'll try."

~

"Thanks, Breytenbach," says Susman into De Villiers' phone. "We're on our way."

"M1 South," says De Villiers. "Where the hell is he going?"

"Trying to leave the province?"

"Maybe."

"Where would you go?" asks Susman.

"I don't know. Maybe a sleepy seaside town? Maybe somewhere that's not that easily accessible. But I wouldn't try to cross a border. Too risky."

"Wild Coast?"

"That would be a good choice. A place like Port St Johns. You could definitely disappear there."

"Please don't tell me we're driving to the Transkei tonight."

"Why not?" says De Villiers. "I could do with a *fokken* holiday."

Susman thinks for a while. "You know what? He won't have the patience for a long trip. I bet you he's thinking of stopping if he hasn't stopped already."

"What's in the south?"

"I don't know. Soweto? Nasrec? Discount furniture? Mine dumps?

Gold Reef City?"

"Gold Reef City. Ha," says De Villiers. "Destination to generations of serial killers."

"Hold on," says Susman, her brain ticking over.

"Hmm?"

"You said generations of serial killers."

"I was kidding," says De Villiers. "It's an amusement park. It was a joke."

"I know," she says, not smiling. "What about ... hold on."

She speed-dials Khaya. "Hey, Khaya. Where did Flock grow up?"

"Jo'burg," he says. "And then the Bergview Boys Home."

"Where in Jo'burg?"

"Uh ... I can't remember off the top of my head. Let me grab the file."

"In the south?" asks Susman.

"Affirmative. I mean they moved around a bit when their circumstances changed, depending on if they had money or not. But they stayed in that area."

"Was there a family home? Or a house Flock would think of as a family home?"

She hears Khaya paging through the file.

"Here it is," he says. "House owned by Brenda Flock ... definitely in the south."

"Bingo," says Susman.

"Here we go. Rosettenville. 58 Arcadia Avenue."

"'That's close. We're close."

"Double bingo," says De Villiers.

"You guys are there?" asks Khaya. "I'm sweating on this side."

"You and me, both. My hands are slipping on this steering wheel. Call the current owner of that house to warn them. Send back-up. See you later."

"One more thing," says Khaya. "We got an ID on the woman he took from the park."

"Yes?"

"Sarah Stillwell. Reported missing ten minutes ago by her boyfriend. Not home, not answering her phone."

"Sarah," says Susman. *We are on our way. Hang in there. Fight for your life.*

"What took him so long?"

"Denial. He said she doesn't fit the profile on the news: not single, not a brunette. But she took their infant son to the park, and she didn't come home. He's on his way to the station to get the baby."

"Flock picked Stillwell out of his usual profile because he's desperate," says Susman. "Desperate killers make me very nervous."

The suburb is quiet. David Flock carries the unconscious body of Sarah Stillwell up to the front gate of the old house and rings the intercom bell. Her face is still scented by the second application of chloroform: sweet and dry.

A Greek man answers, his voice is immediately suspicious. They've recently experienced a spike in crime, and he knows to be careful. "Hello? Who's there?"

"Help!" beseeches Flock.

"Who's there?"

"Please! Help!" Flock yells. "I've been attacked! They hurt my girlfriend!"

"Who are you?"

"Please! We need help! We need an ambulance!"

The man pauses, then buzzes the gate open. Flock stumbles in, still playing the part.

"Oh, thank you! Oh!"

"Oh my God!" says the homeowner. "What happened?"

"They tried to hijack us."

"Who?"

"Two men. Came out from nowhere. Lock the door!"

The man locks the front door and bolts it.

"Here," he says, showing Flock the couch. "Lay her down here. I'll call the ambulance."

"Taki? Taki?" comes a woman's voice from the other side of the house. "What's going on?"

"Call an ambulance, Evelina!"

"Why? What's wrong?" She arrives in the room and gasps loudly. She's drying her hands on the front of her apron. "Oh, God! What happened? Who is she? What's wrong with her?" She rushes to Sarah's side and feels her cheek.

"Call the ambulance, love," says Taki. "And the police. Please."

The phone rings and the Greek couple appear confused.

"Is there anyone else in the house?" asks Flock.

"No," Taki replies, frowning. "Why?"

Flock pulls out his gun and shoots Taki, then Evelina. The gunshots are like thunder. It jolts Sarah; she groans, then goes back to sleep.

"Look. Look," says Flock. He shakes Sarah and slaps her cheeks.

Sarah struggles to open her eyes. She can smell gunpowder and blood, and the ground is moving beneath her.

"Look, Mother," Flock says. "We're home."

Swanepoel's car radio crackles.

"Shots fired," says De Villiers.

"Shots? At the house?" asks Breytenbach.

"Neighbours called it in," says De Villiers. "Occupants not answering their phone."

"It's him," says Breytenbach. "It must be him."

"Tell Devil we're close," says Swanepoel. "We can be there in—"

"We're minutes away," says Breytenbach into the radio. "Maybe five."

"Good," says the detective. "It's Go Time."

"You wearing vests?" asks Breytenbach.

"Always," replies Devil.

"See you there."

37

A FILTHY DRESSING GOWN

FLOCK LEVERS SARAH'S weak body up off the couch. "I'm taking you to your special chair, Mother."

Sarah is terrified. She wants to scream that she is not his mother.

"You remember your special chair?" he asks.

She can hardly speak. Her mouth is so dry that swallowing is painful. She searches for a way out, but all the windows have burglar bars. She needs to see the rest of the house. Find a small window, a back door. "Why don't you ... why don't you show me that cupboard? The cupboard your mother used to put you in."

"I won't go in there again!" shouts Flock.

"Of course not." Her voice is a croak. "Of course not. No one will go into the cupboard again. I want you to show me."

"I'll show you the Special Chair," he says.

"Okay," says Sarah.

They arrive in a small living room.

"It used to be in here," he says, growing agitated. "Someone's taken it."

"There are ... there were other people living here. It's not your mom's house anymore."

"I need the Special Chair. You have to sit in the Special Chair."

"Here's a chair," says Sarah. "Look. We can use this one."

"That's not the Special Chair," he says. His eyes are black.

Sarah gets spooked but holds her nerve. "We can pretend."

"The Special Chair has a leash," he says. "And locks."

"Locks?"

"Sit," he says, and Sarah has no choice but to do so. Flock rummages in the bag he has brought along and brings out cable ties and rope. He ties Sarah to the chair.

"You don't need to tie me up," Sarah says. "I won't leave you."

"They all leave," he says.

"Your mom used to lock you ... in your Special Chair?"

"It was my fault," he says.

"She'd lock you in as a punishment?"

"I didn't like it when the men came to visit."

"The ... men?"

"The men would come, and I would run into her bedroom to stop them from touching her. From taking her goodness away. Stealing her light."

"So she kept you here when she had ... visitors?"

"The visitors brought money. Without money, we didn't eat. They took her light and gave us money."

"She did it because she loved you," says Sarah.

"She did it because she wanted to control me. She wanted to see me locked up."

"That's terrible. I would never do that to my little boy."

"I know. I've been watching you."

Sarah's breath is knocked out of her. "How do you know?"

"I saw you singing to your baby. Talking to him. I can see your goodness. It leaks out of you like light. Like the sun behind a tree. You are a Real Mother. No cruelty. No s-sordid acts. I saw your glow, and that's why I took you."

"But then why are you doing this to me? Why hurt me? Take me away from my baby?"

Flock chooses not to hear her. "Enough talking now. We need to finish what we started." He's finished securing her to the chair. He checks the tension of the rope and seems happy with it.

"Let's just talk," says Sarah. "Let's talk for one more minute. I want to know more about you."

He locks eyes with her. "It won't work."

Ice chinks down her spine. "What won't work?"

"I know you're trying to buy time. I don't blame you."

"I care about you," says Sarah. "I want to—"

"No, Mommy. No. You don't."

Flock unpacks the rest of his bag, and Sarah is so horrified by what she sees, she almost loses control of her bladder. "What are those things?" she whispers. "Why did you bring them?"

"They took my first mother away. Then I made a new one, and they took that one away too. They're not going to take you away."

"I never locked you in a cupboard. I never fastened you to a chair. I'm not your mother."

"Not yet," says Flock, "but you will be."

"What do you mean?"

"I brought my tools. I'll make you look like her. And then I'll take you like I always wanted to take her."

Sarah's entire body shakes. "No," she says. "Please."

"It was my right to take her light, you see? To take her whole light, to take her life. But they robbed me of that chance. So now it's my turn. I'm taking what is rightfully mine."

He pulls a large knife out of a sheath.

"No," pleads Sarah. "Please. I'll do anything."

"I've sharpened it. Especially for you."

Sarah can't think of anything else to say. She weeps.

"But first: hair. Dark hair, like this." He pulls a wig onto her head and seems pleased with the results. "Yes," he says. "It looks good. Being a brunette suits you." He grabs her face, and she cries out. "But your eyes are wrong. Mother had green eyes. They should be green. Hold still." He tries to put contact lenses into her eyes, but she fights him.

"No!" she shouts.

He squeezes her cheeks tighter, trying to keep her still, but he can't force her eyes open and keep her head still at the same time.

"Hold still!" he shouts. "It won't hurt. They're contact lenses!"

Sarah keeps fighting, moving her head out of his grasp. "No!"

Flock loses his temper and slaps her as hard as he can. The whole chair tips over with the force of the blow. As Sarah falls with the chair, she hits her head on the floor, cracking her skull, which lights up with white-hot pain. Flock hauls the chair upright again, and Sarah is barely conscious. He holds the knife up to her eye socket. "Now, you hold still, or I'll take your pretty blue eyes right out. You choose— contact lenses, or the knife."

This time, she doesn't stop him putting the lenses in.

"There. Green eyes. That looks good. We're almost done."

He puts the knife down and applies make-up. "Now, you need to stop crying, or you'll smudge it."

The little energy she has oozes out of her body.

"Sing that song to me," he murmurs.

"What?" mumbles Sarah. She can hardly talk, never mind sing. "Which song?"

"The one you were singing to your baby at the park." He waits for her to start, but there is a sound on the road. "Did you hear that?" he whispers.

She shakes her head, and the agony of it makes her grimace. "No," she whispers back. "I didn't hear anything."

"We need to hurry. They're going to take you away from me again. I need to—"

He grabs his knife, and a chill runs through Sarah. She swallows a scream.

"No, they won't!" Her voice is an urgent whisper. "No one knows we're here. Put the knife down. You don't need it yet."

"You don't understand," he hisses. "They have eyes everywhere."

"Who?"

"The Parable People," says Flock. "God watches through their eyes. He sees everything."

"We're all alone, can't you see? You can take your time. Make sure the moment is perfect. Don't rush it."

"I know what you're trying to do," he says with a sneer. "I'm not stupid."

"What about my clothes? I'm wearing shorts and a T-shirt. That's not right, is it? What would your mother be wearing?"

Flock thinks for a moment. "A dressing gown," he says. "A filthy dressing gown."

She blinks at him. "Should we look for a nice dress? I'm sure there must be one in the house." Her wrist strains against the rope. Sarah tries to hold out her hand to him as a mother would to a small child. If he unties her from the chair, she'll be able to lead him into a different room.

"Don't move," says Flock. His voice is a razor. He forces the knife against her stomach, and she doubles over in fright. There is a ripping sound, a tearing of fabric. She thinks he has cut her open and sobs silently. When she opens her eyes, she sees he has cut her clothes off. She sits there, bent over, vulnerable in her underwear. There is so much skin on show: skin he'll use for his own purposes. Flock looks pleased. "There. Now you look like her. Exactly like her. I think you're ready."

"Here," says Susman. "Kill your lights. Park here. We'll walk up to the house. I don't want to force his hand."

De Villiers switches off the car's headlights and parks quietly in the street a few houses down from what used to be the Flock family house.

"Susman," says De Villiers. "Don't take this the wrong way—"

"I'm not staying in the car, Devil. No way."

"Please, Susman. You know I'm not asking because you're a ... a woman. You're a better cop than most men I know."

She shoots him a lethal look. *"Most* men?" She cocks her gun and flicks off the safety switch.

"Okay," he says. "You're a better cop than *any of the men* I know. I'm asking because you don't need any more danger—any more trauma—in your life. It will get messy in there. Let me do it."

"No, De Villiers. I need this. I need to do this."

They stop whispering and pad up to the house.

"Well, it was worth a try," he murmurs.

"Was it?" she asks.

"Yes. At least the major can't fire me."

They share a rare grin. "This is the house," Susman says.

Devil nods. "I'll go round the back."

38

SPILL HER LIGHT

"IT'S time to say goodbye, Mother."

"No, please," says Sarah. "Please, think of my baby."

His breath deepens and slows; his eyes become glassy. "I have dreamt of this moment for so long. I've planned it over and over, and now it's here."

"Please," she chokes. "My baby needs me. If you let me go, I won't tell anyone."

"I want you to remember all the times you hurt me," he says. "Hurt your little boy."

"I never hurt you!" she says. "I wouldn't!"

"All the times you locked me in the cupboard. Strapped me into the Special Chair."

"Please don't," begs Sarah. "It's hurting me. Look, I'm bleeding."

They both look at her stomach, where the knife has drawn a thin line of blood.

"I want you to remember how you punched me, how you burnt me with your cigarettes. I have scars all over my body. I see them—I see you—every time I look in a mirror."

"I'm sorry," Sarah sobs. "I'm so sorry."

"Do you remember what you said to me when you burnt my face?" He bites his bottom lip as if he is in pain. He doesn't fight the tears.

"I'm so sorry for what I did to you," says Sarah. "I was wrong. I love you. You're my special boy. Please don't do this."

Flock grimaces as if he is at war with himself. He slowly pushes the knife deeper.

Suddenly, there's an almighty bang, and De Villiers bursts into the room, shouting at Flock to put down his weapon, aiming his gun directly at the man with the knife.

"Put your hands up!" the detective orders.

Flock freezes in disbelief.

"UP! PUT THEM UP!"

Slowly, quietly, Flock says, "I think you're mistaken."

"I'm not mistaken, David Flock. I know who you are. Now put that knife down, or I'll shoot."

"He's got a g-gun," stammers Sarah. "Hidden." She gestures at his other hand.

"Shut up, bitch," Flock snarls.

"Her name is Sarah," says the detective. "She has a family who love her."

Flock licks his lips nervously. "You shoot me, and she's dead. You'll die, too."

"Put down your weapon, Flock, or I'll send a bullet into your brain so fast—"

"You wouldn't dare, not with her in the firing line."

De Villiers hesitates.

"Now you see the real situation. Put your weapon down."

De Villiers tightens his grip on the gun. "Not a chance."

"Put it down, or this knife goes in."

"No, Flock. You need to—"

Sarah roars in pain as the knife travels deeper into her stomach.

"I'm not bluffing, pig. That's real blood."

"Okay," says the detective, putting his hands up in a show of surrender. "Okay, okay, I'm putting it down." He lays his gun on the floor.

"Kick it away from you," says Flock. His eyes are dead swamps.

De Villiers swipes at the gun with his shoe, and it slides across the wooden floor.

"Now handcuff yourself to that furniture." Flock gestures with a flick of his chin at a nearby three-seater couch.

When the detective hesitates, Sarah screams in agony again, creating a bright flash in De Villiers' mind. He has visions of how Robin Susman had been tortured by the Turbine Hall Gang, even though he hadn't been there to witness it. His secret is that he had seen the files, had seen the photos. Of course he had, they just pretended, between them, that he hadn't. It was too intimate, examining the medical report photographs — the broken bones, internal bleeding, the emergency hysterectomy that saved her from bleeding out.

Sarah screams again, jolting De Villiers into action.

"Okay!" he yells. "I'm doing it. I'm doing it."

With shaking fingers, he handcuffs himself to the backbone of the large couch.

"Keys," demands Flock. His face is as lifeless as his eyes now; just a mask hiding the pain and evil within. De Villiers lobs his keys to Flock, who is pleased. "There. That's better."

Sarah's terror is unbearable. De Villiers forces himself to look; makes himself bear witness to what one human will do to another. It's the least he can do.

Flock wipes Sarah's tears and strokes her wig. "Hush, Mother," he whispers into her ear. "This will all be over soon."

Sarah doubles over again, weeping. He forces her body back against the chair.

"Now, Mommy," he says. "I want you to watch as the knife goes in. I want you to see all your light spilling out because it's a beautiful thing to see."

Sarah shrieks and kicks, fighting against the rope and her attacker.

"No," says De Villiers. "We had a deal!"

Flock looks at the detective with disdain. "There was no deal."

De Villiers thrashes against his cuffs to free himself, knowing it's impossible to break the chain.

"Help!" gasps Sarah. "Help!"

Flock slaps her bruised cheek to keep her quiet, but she will not.

"Shut up!" he shouts into her face, spit flying. "I'm taking your light from you. I want you to watch me taking all the light back."

"Leave her alone you son of a bitch!" shouts De Villiers. "You coward! You Mommy's Boy!"

Flock's eyes flare. "What did you just say?" He leaves Sarah—scrambling to dislodge her binding—and walks over to De Villiers, gun pointed at his chest, finger on the trigger.

A calm female voice arrives. "David," she says.

Flock spins around and sees Susman. "Who the—"

"I'm a friend," she says. "Here. Here's my gun."

She slides her gun along the floor to Flock. De Villiers blinks the sweat out of his eyes.

"Take it," Susman says. "It's proof that I mean you no harm."

"I don't have friends," says Flock.

"Your mother sent me," says Susman.

"My mother is dead."

"I have a message for you."

"Shut up," Flock says, pointing his weapon at her.

"She said to tell you: *Vlokkie*, I love you."

He looks at Susman as if he has seen a ghost. His nostrils flare. "Who are you?

"She said she's sorry she hurt you."

"I won't let you," he says. "I won't let you take this away from me."

"You need not take anything," says Susman in a loving, lilting voice. "You have what you need."

"I need to take the light," says Flock.

"You already have the light," says Susman. "It's inside you."

"There's no light inside me," he cries. "Just black. She took the light away from me."

"You know, *Vlokkie*. I have lots of light inside of me."

He stares at her. "Do you? I don't see it. Usually, I can see it."

"I do," says Susman. "Much more than the girl in the chair."

"No, Susman!" shouts De Villiers. "Don't do it!" He refuses to allow Susman to sacrifice herself again.

Susman appears as unruffled as De Villiers has ever seen her. "Why don't you let Sarah go, and take my light instead?"

"But I've prepared her," says Flock. "She's ready."

"She's not ready," says Susman. "Look at her. She's petrified. You won't get any light out of her."

"You're trying to trick me."

"No. Put down your gun and I'll show you."

"I don't know you. It's a trick."

"Brenda sent me," says Susman. "I am unarmed. Nothing bad can happen."

He hesitates.

"Look here." She takes off her Kevlar vest and her shirt. The sound of Velcro tearing open is loud in the tense room. Susman's torso is a testament to her ordeal at the hands of the brutal gang: scars run in every direction. De Villiers winches his eyes closed.

Flock is in awe. "You're ... you're like me. The scars..." He drops his gun.

"These scars are special. It's how you get the light out. Pass me the knife. I'll show you."

Flock is mesmerised. He passes her the knife and waits with an open mouth to see Susman spill her light. He moves closer; just close enough for Susman to grip the knife as hard as she can and turn it on Flock, forcing it as far into his stomach as she can, and twisting it.

Instead of roaring in anger, which Susman expected him to do, he groans as if in rapture. His face seems peaceful at last. He looks at her as he falls back.

"Watch out," shouts De Villiers. "Gun!"

Flock had fallen next to his gun. He grabs it and points it at Susman. "Your turn."

Susman dives out of the bullet's trajectory as he fires.

Breytenbach and Swanepoel crash into the room.

"Drop it!" shouts Swanepoel. Flock lies on the floor, blood pouring from his stomach and his mouth. Slowly, he gets to his feet. He doesn't lower his gun.

"Drop your weapon, Flock," yells Breytenbach. "It's over."

Flock lifts his gun for the last time, his fingers slippery with blood. Swanepoel fires, as does Flock. Susman dives at Sarah, crashing the chair to the floor and trying to untie the rope with numb, shaking fingers. There are shouts of pain, and Susman looks up. Adrenaline zips through her body. Both Flock and Breytenbach have caught a bullet; both men fall and drop their guns. Although Flock seems to no longer be a threat, Swanepoel clenches his jaw and pulls the trigger three times, sending a further trio of shells into the killer's chest. He walks over and checks Flock's pulse and appears satisfied.

He kneels next to the injured lieutenant. "Breytenbach."

Breytenbach looks confused. "What?"

"You've been hit," says Swanepoel.

"Did I get him?" he asks. There is blood on his lips.

"You're bleeding," says Swanepoel. "Don't move." He rips the walkie-talkie from his belt and talks into it. "Officer down, officer down!"

Breytenbach smiles, and more blood spills from his mouth. He looks sleepy.

Swanepoel squeezes his hand. "Stay with me, Breyts."

Devil looks over at Susman. "Robin, you okay?"

She nods. "I'm okay."

"The keys for the cuffs are in his pocket."

Susman roots in Flock's pocket and unlocks De Villiers' handcuffs, which have bitten into his wrists and left bloody welts.

Sarah, now free of her restraints, is bawling in relief. Even if she could talk, they wouldn't be able to hear her over the cacophony of sirens arriving outside.

"Swanepoel, did I get him?" asks Breytenbach, gurgling.

"Yes, Breyts. You got him."

"Flock ... Dead?"

"Yes. Dead. He's dead. You got him."

Breytenbach exhales and closes his eyes.

"Hang on, man, hang on. Hey! The medics are on their way."

EPILOGUE

EVERLASTING

PARKVIEW POLICE STATION, **18th of July 2014, 09:28.**

The Parkview Police Station has a light atmosphere the morning after finding David Flock. There is chatting and laughing at the open-plan desks and coffee station.

Msibi sashays in.

"My trio! My tribe! How is everyone on this wonderful morning? I heard all about last night. What brio! What bravery! I'm proud to call you my team."

De Villiers smiles at her.

"Couldn't have done it without you," says Susman. "You're still the best forensic I know."

"*Ja*, well, I'm guessing my pay raise is in the post?" She laughs uproariously at her own joke. "Hey! Talking about pay raises and promotions, where is my favourite cop? My beautiful Breytenbach?"

"Hey," says Khaya, feigning sorrow. "I thought I was your favourite!"

Msibi laughs again. "Well, if Breyts hadn't survived his gunshot wound you would be, my little sausage dog."

"He's out of surgery and in ICU," says Swanepoel. "It wasn't looking good for him, but this morning his doctor said he's out of the woods."

"Thank God for that! We should give him a medal or something. Or maybe something more useful than a medal. Talking of which, Devil, you still owe me a beer."

"Well, while we're handing out complimentary beers," says De Villiers. "We'd do well to give one to Susman, too, for her excellent work last night."

Susman shakes her head, dismissing the compliment.

De Villiers insists. "We'd all be chilling in your morgue, Msibi, if it weren't for her." He turns to look at Robin. "I mean it, Susman. You were ... brilliant. Brilliant. I've never seen a cop keep their cool like you did."

Susman, not enjoying being the centre of attention, deflects the praise. "And De Villiers, and Khaya, and Swanepoel ... and that pesky journalist ... what's her name?"

"Walker!" says Swanepoel. "I need to call her about Paviel. Okay, boss?"

De Villiers nods, and Swanepoel dials Walker's number.

"And that mother?" asks Msibi. "Was she okay?"

"Superficial injuries only, but staying in the hospital for observation. Reunited with her baby boy last night," replies Susman. "It was ... touching."

Jennifer Walker answers the phone, her voice sultry. "Well, hello, lieutenant."

"Hello my lovely," he says.

"Hmm. No more Sweet Lips?"

"You've graduated."

"Ah. We're taking this seriously now?"

"Well, I'd like to take you out for dinner tonight to discuss it, if you're free."

"I'm all yours," says Walker. "I'll wear something pretty."

"No need."

"Oh my," she laughs. "Is it that kind of dinner?"

Swanepoel laughs. "No, what I meant is ... anything on you looks pretty. You'd look good wearing sackcloth."

"See you tonight, then?"

"Actually, I'd like to see you sooner than that."

"Hmm?"

"Devil agreed that your tip-off last night was key to finding the Jigsaw Killer."

"I just got lucky," she says.

"As a reward, he said you can get an exclusive with Paviel. He's the co-accused in the Sterling Safari murder case."

"I know who he is!" says Walker. "Do you think he'll speak to me?"

"He handed himself in this morning—virtually foaming at the mouth—he's so angry that Sterling snitched on him. He wants to shout his story from the rooftops. I told him I knew just the journalist he should speak to."

After the call, Swanepoel returns to the group. They're laughing at the punchline to a joke he arrives too late to catch. Susman sneaks away. Suddenly, they stop chuckling. They're looking at the woman who has just arrived.

"Anna-Mart!" says De Villiers. He rushes to her, embraces her, takes her aside. The officers greet her politely in Afrikaans. *Goeiemôre, Mevrou* De Villiers.

"You've been crying," murmurs De Villiers.

"It feels so strange ... to be back here, at the station."

"I know I was supposed to see you last night, but we got a break on the case and—"

"I know, André. I know. Police work always comes first."

"It was three a.m. when we finished, and I didn't want to wake you."

"It doesn't matter."

"It matters! Of course it matters."

"I mean, it doesn't matter, truly," says Anna-Mart. "Nothing matters except that Niel is alive."

De Villiers dares to hope. "Niel? Are you sure? How do you know?"

"He just phoned me. Can you imagine? He just phoned me. I thought I'd never hear his voice again and there he was, saying 'Hi Ma' as if I'd seen him just yesterday." The detective is speechless, and they embrace again. "He was travelling, didn't even know they had bombed his kibbutz."

Khaya pads over to them. "I'm sorry to interrupt, sir. The major wants us in his office immediately."

De Villiers is reluctant to leave Anna-Mart. "Can't his congratulations wait for a few minutes?"

"No such luck. It's not to congratulate us. It's a new case. The head of Edelweiss Retirement Village has reported suspected homicides—"

"Homicides? Plural? How many?"

"Seven suspicious deaths so far this year. He suspects foul play. Wants us to investigate. That's why Msibi is here. She's calling in the bodies."

"Hell," says the detective, scratching the back of his head.

"The major wants to brief us right now."

"Go," says Anna-Mart.

"Are you sure? See you later?"

"Go save the world, Devil. I'll be at home—our home—waiting for you when you're ready."

The energy is intense in Major Denton's office; the atmosphere is charged with emotional intimacy and things unsaid.

"Please, Robin," says Alastair. "Reconsider?"

"No, Alistair," says Susman. "No way. I'm going home."

"This is your home! You don't belong on a farm."

"How do you know? How do you know where I belong?"

"Without you, the Jigsaw Killer would still be out there. That baby would never have seen his mother again!"

"We don't know that," says Susman, but the implication cuts deep.

"I know that."

"I'm sorry, I just can't. I need to take care of myself. I need to fix my own ... oxygen mask. Oh, never mind."

"It's not just that, Robin. It's more than the work. I want you here because I can protect you here. I can't protect you if you are hundreds of kilometres away." He takes a step towards her.

"I don't need your protection."

"The hell you don't! Mabaleng is out there. The Turbine Hall Gang is out there. They'll go after you. I can't let you leave."

"I have my shotgun," says Susman. "And no one outside of this station knows where my farm is."

He sighs and pauses a moment. "If you insist on being obstinate—"

"Oh yes, how dare I insist on having my own life?" says Susman.

"If you insist on going back, then I will send a bodyguard with you, to that Godforsaken farm."

"The farm is the opposite of 'Godforsaken'," says Susman. "There is peace there, and miracles. Even to a hardened old atheist like me, there is divinity in everything. Not like here."

"You'll agree to have a bodyguard, then?"

"It depends," says Susman.

"On what?"

"On who he is. Is he any good with sheep? I can always do with an extra farm-hand."

"Robin, be serious."

"I am being serious. If I am to be tailed day in and day out like a shark with a pilot fish, there will have to be an up-side. Also: can he pour good Martinis?"

"You're impossible."

The remark makes them both stop, then Robin speaks quietly. "That's what you always used to say."

"Well," says the major gruffly. "You haven't changed."

Susman offers him a sad smile. "If only that were true."

"Robin. I feel like if I let you go—"

"You mean if you let me go *again*—"

The major is pained, and his mouth turns down. "That I'll never see you again. I can't abide that idea."

Susman shakes her head. "It's too late. Don't you see it's too late? Too late for me with my torn up insides and too late for you with your pretty wife and baby. Too late for us."

Alastair exclaims in dismay. They are so close they're almost touching. "You know that I'd leave her in an instant if I could be with you."

"Don't say that," pleads Robin. "Don't say that. It's not fair to anyone."

There is a tap on the door, and they reluctantly move apart.

"Major, sir?" says Khaya, through the door. "I've gathered the team."

The major clears his throat, straightens his tie, and takes his seat behind the desk.

"You said ... you said tulips are no longer your favourite flowers."

"That's right," says Susman, gathering her things.

"Which are now? Your favourites?"

"Everlastings. They're indigenous grassland blooms."

"May I send you some when I think of you?" asks the major.

"There's no need. They grow wild all over my farm."

Robin and Clementine are travelling on the dirt road leading up to Robin's farm.

"We're almost there," says Susman. "Take the next right. And thanks again for driving me."

"I wouldn't have had it any other way! Four uninterrupted hours to gab to my very best friend. Luxury!"

She brakes slowly and turns.

"It hasn't been all bad," says Susman.

"What do you mean, all bad? You rocked the city! You simply dazzled!"

Susman looks out of the window. "I wouldn't go that far. Mostly, it was teamwork."

"Alistair said you were absolutely incredible."

Susman chuckles. "I've never heard my name and the word 'dazzle' in the same sentence before."

"Doesn't make it untrue. Have the nightmares stopped?"

"They have, actually. I had six hours of uninterrupted sleep last night. I can't remember the last time that happened."

"That's wonderful."

"Here we are! My farm. I'm still not used to saying that." The luxury SUV slows down and turns into a gravel driveway. "I need to think of a name for it. Put up a sign. It's time. I'll call it Everlasting."

"That sounds perfect, really. Happy to be home?"

"More than happy. Back to the land. This is the first time it's felt like home," says Susman, opening the window and sniffing the air. "Can you smell that? That beautiful fresh country air?"

"All I can smell is wild grass and ... dung."

"Yes, well, it's kind of the same thing. Literally."

Clementine parks the vehicle, and they climb out. Sheep bleat in the distance.

"What will do you about the lambs?" asks Clementine. "The poor precious lambs? How will you cope with sending them to the abattoir?"

"I won't be sending them anywhere," says Susman. "They will remain alive and well under my amateur shepherding skills. Their very fleece fibres are numbered."

"Come again?"

"There aren't going to be lamb chops on this menu. Khaya assured me that Merinos—that's the breed of sheep I have—make excellent wool."

∼

THE END

DEAR READER

Thank you for supporting my work!

If you're ready for more Devil & Susman stories, you can find them in my *Sticky Fingers* collection, where we dive deeper with their characters while they solve missing person cases.

The following are Devil & Susman stories:

1. *Panama Wings* (Sticky Fingers 2)

2. *Sky Mirror* (Sticky Fingers 3)

3. *The Green Silk Scarf* (Sticky Fingers 4)

4. *The Generation of Lost Girls* (Sticky Fingers 5)

5. *Home-made Coffin* (Sticky Fingers 6)

The *Sticky Fingers* stories are perfect for fans of Gillian Flynn and Roald Dahl, and are guaranteed to get under your skin.

* * *

"Lawrence makes every word count, telling each story with elegance and emotional punch." — Patsy Hennessey

"Each story is masterfully constructed ... Humorous, touching, creepy, but most of all entertaining, this collection is superb." — Tracy Michelle Anderson

* * *

I love hearing from readers. If you'd like to contact me, I'm just an email away.

Thank you again for supporting my work, and happy reading!

Janita

janita@firefinchpress.com

www.jt-lawrence.com

ALSO BY JT LAWRENCE

≈

FICTION

SCI-FI THRILLER
WHEN TOMORROW CALLS
• SERIES •

The Stepford Florist: A Novelette

The Sigma Surrogate

1. Why You Were Taken
2. How We Found You
3. What Have We Done

When Tomorrow Calls Box Set: Books 1 - 3

≈

URBAN FANTASY

BLOOD MAGIC SERIES

1. The HighFire Crown
2. The Dream Drinker
3. The Witch Hunter

4. The Ember Isles

5. The Chaos Jar

6. The New Dawn Throne

STANDALONE NOVELS

The Memory of Water

Grey Magic

SHORT STORY COLLECTIONS

Sticky Fingers

Sticky Fingers 2

Sticky Fingers 3

Sticky Fingers 4

Sticky Fingers 5

Sticky Fingers 6

Sticky Fingers: 36 Deliciously Twisted Short Stories: The Complete Box Set
Collection (Books 1 - 3)

NON-FICTION

The Underachieving Ovary

ABOUT THE AUTHOR

JT Lawrence is a USA Today bestselling author and playwright. She lives in Parkview, Johannesburg, in a house with a red front door.

www.jt-lawrence.com
janita@pulpbooks.co.za

Made in the USA
Monee, IL
20 December 2019